A VOICE FOR THE PEOPLE

A VOICE FOR THE PEOPLE

The Life and Work of Harold Courlander

NINA JAFFE

HENRY HOLT AND COMPANY • NEW YORK

Henry Holt and Company, Inc., *Publishers since 1866*
115 West 18th Street, New York, New York 10011

Henry Holt is a registered trademark of Henry Holt and Company, Inc.

Published in Canada by Fitzhenry & Whiteside Ltd.,
195 Allstate Parkway, Markham, Ontario L3R 4T8.

Library of Congress Cataloging-in-Publication Data
Jaffe, Nina.
A voice for the people: the life and work of Harold Courlander / Nina Jaffe.
p. cm.
Includes bibliographical references and index.
Summary: A biography of the folklorist and novelist who recorded the traditional songs and stories of the people of Haiti, the Hopi Indians, and black communities in the South, connecting the African-American traditions to the cultures of Africa.
1. Courlander, Harold, 1908–1996—Juvenile literature.
2. Folklorists—United States—Biography—Juvenile literature.
3. Afro-Americans—Folklore. 4. Folklore—Caribbean Area.
5. Folklore—Africa. 6. Indians of North America—Southwest, New—Folklore.
[1. Courlander, Harold, 1908–1996. 2. Folklorists. 3. Authors, American.
4. Afro-Americans—Folklore. 5. Folklore—United States.
6. Folklore—Caribbean Area. 7. Folklore—Africa.] I. Title.
GR55.C68J33 1997 398'.092—dc20 [B] 96-32513 CIP AC

ISBN 0-8050-3444-7
First Edition—1997
Printed in the United States of America on acid-free paper. ∞
10 9 8 7 6 5 4 3 2 1

Book design by Debbie Glasserman

The author is grateful to the following for permission to reprint selected materials from Harold Courlander's publications:

Excerpts from *The Master of the Forge: A West African Odyssey* copyright © 1983, 1996 by Harold Courlander and *The Bordeaux Narrative* copyright © 1990 by Harold Courlander, courtesy of Marlowe Publishing Co. The reprinting of "Bouqui and Ti Malice Go Fishing" and the lyrics to the song beginning "Jésus, Marie, Joseph, oh" from *The Drum and the Hoe: Life and Lore of the Haitian People* copyright © 1960 by Harold Courlander. Excerpts from "Recollections of Haiti in the 1930's and 40's" courtesy of *African Arts* (1990).

Excerpts from *Haiti* copyright © 1939 by University of North Carolina Press, copyright © 1967 by Harold Courlander; *The Caballero* copyright © 1940, 1967 by Harold Courlander; *The Big Old World of Richard Creeks* copyright © 1962 by Harold Courlander; *The Hat-Shaking Dance and Other Ashanti Tales from Ghana* copyright © 1957, 1985 by Harold Courlander; and *The African* copyright © 1967, 1993 by Harold Courlander; abridged reprintings of "The Four Worlds" from *The Fourth World of the Hopis* copyright © 1971 by Harold Courlander, the title story of *Terrapin's Pot of Sense* copyright © 1957, 1985 by Harold Courlander; and the lyrics and musical notation of "Baby Please Don't Go" from *Negro Folk Music U.S.A.* copyright © 1991 by Harold Courlander.

Excerpts from *On Recognizing the Human Species* (1960) courtesy of Anti-Defamation League.

Excerpts from "How I Got My Log Cabin" (1991) courtesy of *Chronicle: The Quarterly Magazine of the Historical Society of Michigan*. Excerpts from "Recording in Alabama in the 1950's" (1985), "Recording on a Hopi Reservation, 1968–1981" (1990), and "Recording in Eritrea in 1942–43" (1987) courtesy of *Resound: A Quarterly of the Archives of Traditional Music.* Excerpts from "Notes from an Abyssinian Diary" (1944) courtesy of Oxford University Press. Excerpts from "The Emperor Wore Clothes: Visiting Haile Selassie in 1943" (1989) courtesy of *American Scholar.*

Excerpt from Courlander's correspondence with Melville Herskovits courtesy of Northwestern University Archives and the reprinting of a letter to Wynn Stephansen dated 1943 courtesy of Smithsonian/Folkways Archives.

Reprint of "The Scholars and the Lion" from *The Tiger's Whisker and Other Tales from Asia and the Pacific* copyright © 1959, 1987 by Harold Courlander and "The Game Board" from *The Fire on the Mountain and Other Ethiopian Stories* copyright © 1950 by Henry Holt and Company, Inc., copyright © 1995 by Harold Courlander and Wolf Leslau.

For the spirit that keeps us singing—

for Harold

CONTENTS

CONTENTS

ACKNOWLEDGMENTS

I am indebted to many people who helped to make this book possible. I especially wish to thank Robert Baron, Director of the Folk Arts Division at the New York State Council on the Arts; Paddy Bowman, coordinator of the National Task Force on Folk Arts in Education; Stephanie Smith and Jeff Place, archivists at the Smithsonian/Folkways Archives; Joe Hickerson, Director of the Archive of Folk Culture at the American Folklife Center at the Library of Congress; Lois Wilcken, Ethnomusicologist at Hunter College in New York City; and Anthony Seeger, Director of the Center for Folklife Programs and Cultural Studies at the Smithsonian Institution.

Much appreciation also to Marilyn Graf, editor of *Resound: A Quarterly of the Archives of Traditional Music* at Indiana University; Dr. Thomas Kappner, adjunct associate professor of Latin American and Caribbean Studies at City College of New York/CUNY; the research staff at the Bentley Historical Society of Michigan University and Northwestern University Archives; to Beth Posner and the

library staff at Bank Street College of Education; to Sheila Callaghan; and especially to Sharon Cohen, reference librarian and instructor at Queens College School of Library Sciences in New York City.

My colleagues Joseph Kleinman, Cheryl Trobriani, and Linda Levine at Bank Street College of Education generously shared with me their time and resources during the research process. Ina Raikkonnen transcribed numerous hours of interview sessions, and Maritza Charles assisted in typing and organization of reference material. Thanks also to Matoakah Little Eagle of the Thunderbird Dance Company, Lucrece Louisdohn, storyteller and Assistant Director of Children's Programs at the Queensborough Public Library, and composer Fred Ho for their invaluable artistic and cultural perspectives; also to writer and oral historian Cindy Cohen, and to Maxine Davis.

Michael Courlander provided support and important factual details as well as many of the photographs from Harold Courlander's estate. This book could not have been completed without his generous assistance. Thanks also to my editor, Marc Aronson, and to assistant editor Matt Rosen. To my dearest friends Judy David and Doug Leavens; Don Ostrow, Kathy McNamara, and Thea Stone; to my husband, Bob, for his love, patience, and support; and especially to my son, Louis, for helping me keep my eye on the ball. This book belongs to all of them.

PREFACE

This book is about the life of Harold Courlander, a wonderful writer and storyteller. It is also a book about memories. While researching and writing it, I was lucky enough to have the chance to meet and work with Harold Courlander. He told me many stories of his life. He shared many memories. I am telling his story, as I understand it, through his words and his writings.

I became interested in telling stories when I was in high school. In college, as I began to learn more about the many oral traditions of the world, I was often drawn to the stories and collections of Harold Courlander. His book *The Hat-Shaking Dance and Other Ashanti Tales from Ghana* provided a wonderful introduction to the tales of Kwaku Anansi, the trickster spider. There was something about his writing that made the words jump off the page. Whenever I told his stories to people from Ghana, they always nodded in appreciation. "Yes, that is the way it is told."

Harold Courlander and a young boy play the *nugarit*—a large kettle-shaped drum—in Mai Debri village, Eritrea, 1942. *(Courtesy Courlander Family)*

It seemed to me that Courlander had found a way of writing with a speaking voice—echoing in English the many tellers who had shaped these stories for generations all around the world. Years later, I met a woman who was just starting out to become a professional storyteller. I asked her what kind of stories she liked to tell. She said, "I don't like to tell the usual fairy tales. I like to tell Courlander's stories."

Courlander's name is known beyond the circle of storytellers, for he also contributed to our knowledge of the world's musical traditions. After my college years, I also began to study drumming and Afro-Caribbean percussion in New York City. Many of the teachers I worked with knew of Courlander's work. They respected his scholarship and the many recordings he had made for Folkways in Cuba, Haiti, and the Dominican Republic during the 1930s and '40s. His scholarship on Afro-Caribbean religions and books like *Tales of Yoruba Gods and Heroes* also helped students who were trying to learn about the background and meanings behind the songs and rhythms we were studying.

I first met Courlander in the spring of 1994. He lived in a modest brick house in Bethesda, Maryland. I visited him several times, taping our conversations. The transcripts of these tapes, as well as his books and articles and discussions with people who knew him, are the main sources for this book.

Courlander was a teacher in the true sense of the word. Even in his eighties, he was lively and interested in people's stories, histories, current events, and the meanings behind things. He was gentle and kind, yet very, very strong. He reminded me of a tree—sturdy, with many roots and branches, yet able, too, to bend and sway with humor, sympathy, and new ideas.

Harold Courlander died on March 15, 1996. Still his words and his stories live on—in print, in recordings and through the spoken word.

He truly believed in the essential oneness of humanity. He believed that people are linked inextricably to each other through history, to their common past, and to the future. His work has contributed to our way of looking at ourselves, at the world, and each other. I am privileged to share with you what I have learned of his life.

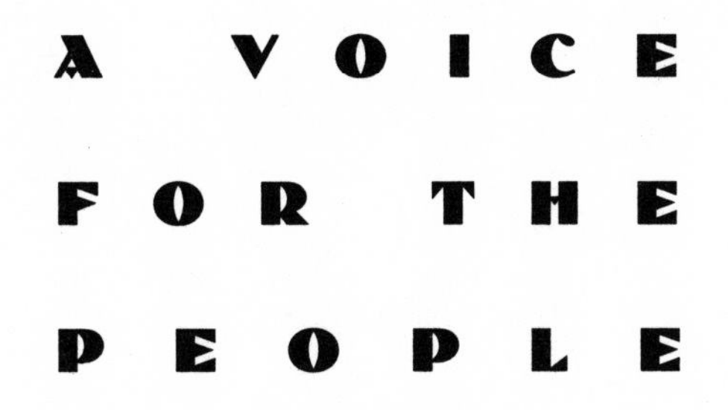
A VOICE
FOR THE
PEOPLE

From The Master of the Forge: A West African Odyssey

Numukeba said: "Great morike, if a story is written, is it not written? Is there nothing more you can tell us?" Mochtar Kidiri pondered, and after a while he said, "We say that a person's story has been written. That we believe it to be so. Yet has the story been written completely? . . . There are gaps in the writing which the person must fill in. . . . Did the Writer of All Stories die after he had written them? No, he is as he was. And if a time comes when the Writer sees that a person has come to a gap in the story, he says to himself, 'At this point my ink ran dry while I was writing. Now, therefore, I will fill in what was not written. Let the person help me write. Let him be aware. Let him decide things. Let him do something. Let him be thoughtful. Let him draw upon the resources of the universe that surround him.' . . . Only when the time comes can a person know his story in all its fullness!"*

* A priest or diviner.

CHAPTER 1

BEGINNINGS

THE SUN WAS BURNING HOT and bright as a tramp ship of the Panama Steamboat Line made its way across the South Atlantic. The boat itself was not remarkable, covered with rusting paint as it chugged through the waters. Sailors on deck swabbed and cleaned, checked the state of the cargo, and coiled up the ropes that lay waterlogged on the wooden planks of the deck. The boat had a passenger, too—a young man with dark hair and far-seeing eyes. Every so often, he would step out on deck to watch the seagulls swoop and dive. He leaned over the prow of the boat and watched the waves pass in swirls and circles. It was 1932. Harold Courlander was on his first trip to Haiti, a trip that would forever change his life, as well as the lives of generations of people whom he met, worked with, and traveled with throughout his long career as a teller of the world's tales.

Courlander's journey began in Indianapolis. He was born on September 18, 1908, the youngest child of Tillie Oppenheim and

Tillie Oppenheim, age 22, and David Courlander, age 29, on their wedding day in 1895. *(Courtesy Courlander Family)*

David Courlander. His parents were both of European Jewish ancestry. His father's family had immigrated from an area called Kurland in Central Europe around 1840. Tillie's family had come from Russia. They lived in England for a time, where Tillie was born, before settling in the United States.

The world that Courlander was born into was very different from the world we live in today. The motorcar was still an oddity. Theodore Roosevelt was president, and the United States was just beginning to emerge as a political force in world politics. In Europe, the Austro-Hungarian Empire stretched over large areas of Central Europe. The Ottoman Empire covered much of Turkey and the Middle East. Russia was ruled by the monarchy of the Romanov family, the czars. Driven by upheavals in Europe—economic hardship, political oppression, famine, and persecution—immigrants from Italy, Poland, Russia, Ireland, and many other countries were pouring into the United States. In Africa and Asia, and across the islands of the Pacific, European countries were carving out territories that they claimed for themselves as colonial "spheres of influence." The British Empire ruled over vast areas of Africa, Asia, and the subcontinent of India. France and Germany were quickly adding

their own colonies in Africa and Asia. Across the United States, cities were growing, but many people lived on small farms across the sweeping plains of the Midwest. In 1908, most Native Americans, from all tribes and nations, had been pushed out of their own lands onto government-owned reservations. Women had not yet achieved the right to vote, and in the schools, everyone was taught to "be an American."

Indianapolis at the time was a bustling midwestern city. As in other parts of America, immigrants from all over Europe were traveling and settling, bringing their hopes, dreams, skills, and knowledge with them. In the burgeoning cities and small towns of farmland and prairie, they mixed with the other groups of Americans who had been there for generations. In Indianapolis, David Courlander set up business as a tailor. It was hard work, but he managed to do well. Harold grew up with his two older sisters, Bertha ("A name she detested," said Courlander, in later years) and Adelaide. While David worked at his business, Tillie cared for the children. One day David heard a knock on the door of his shop. It was his sister Etta. With tears in her eyes, she explained that her husband needed employment. He had a little money to invest. Would David help them out and take her husband in as a partner?

After some hesitation, David Courlander finally agreed and went into business with his brother-in-law. What really happened then no one in the Courlander family knows for sure. Maybe it was dishonesty, or maybe it was just bad investment. Whatever the reason, soon after David took on his new partner, the business failed, and he was left nearly penniless, with nothing to show for all his years of hard work.

"I can start over again," David said to Tillie, "but not here, not in Indianapolis. I want to get out of this town." And so it was that in 1913, when Harold was five years old, he and his family moved to

Detroit, the city that would shape his outlook and sense of the world and its people, for the rest of his life.

▲▲

IN SCHOOL, HAROLD began to mix and mingle with the children from his new Detroit neighborhood. The children were from European countries like Hungary, Poland, and Germany. In the second grade, Harold had his first crush, on a little girl from Hungary. "Every time I saw her," he said, "my knees would shake!" There, too, were the children of black families who had migrated from the farms and small towns of the Deep South. Their parents had come to the industrial North and Midwest as part of the Great Migration, to seek better opportunities for jobs and to leave behind the racist Jim Crow laws, lynchings, and oppressive economic conditions that typified life in the South at that time.

Harold played with everyone, white and black, English-speaking and new immigrants alike. By and large, the children all got along. Perhaps this was because in school they were taught that they were all equal citizens, part of the same democratic society. The idea of America as the great melting pot was the watchword of the public schools. But Harold noticed, too, that children *were* different, depending on where they came from. He was interested in the conversations and stories he heard his black friends tell and share with one another. It seemed to him that there was something special going on—a different language, a different way of thinking about the world, than he knew in his family. And he was curious to learn more.

In 1917, under the leadership of President Woodrow Wilson, the United States entered World War I. This global conflict started in 1914, when Archduke Ferdinand of Austria was gunned down by an

Harold Courlander, age five, after his family had moved to Detroit. *(Courtesy Courlander Family)*

assassin's bullet, setting off a chain of events that ultimately led to the destruction of the Austro-Hungarian, Ottoman, and Russian empires. Thousands of young men volunteered or were called up to serve in the American armed forces. Schools and businesses, factories and farms, were all asked to help with the war effort. On his block, Harold played games with his friends in which they yelled out phrases like "Catch the Kaiser!" as they dashed behind bushes and street lamps. But this was not only a time to play games. Every house in Detroit had a "victory garden." In these gardens, children would grow tomatoes, beans, squash, and carrots. Huge supplies of food were being shipped overseas to help feed American soldiers. The victory gardens were needed to make sure that there would be a continuing supply of food in the cities and small towns across the country. Every contribution, no matter how small, was important. One day in school, the teacher told all the children to bring peach pits for a collection. It was only years later that Harold found out that the peach pits contained a certain chemical important for the manufacture of the protective gear of a gas mask.

During the years of the war, and after it ended, in 1918, the life of the family had to go on. David Courlander began to set up a new tailoring business. But before he could get his feet back on the ground, another disaster struck. David became sick with a debilitating disease that left him weak and bedridden. In those years, the doctors called his condition rheumatoid arthritis, but it was nothing like the arthritis that is known today, and very few treatments were readily available. Things had been hard before, but now the family truly had to scrape by. Still, Harold and his sisters stayed in school, learning to survive as best they could.

Sometimes, in the evenings, David Courlander would begin to spin tales. This he could do, despite his illness. And so he would tell stories—stories from his own imagination, his own yearnings—and

the children would sit and listen. Most of all, he loved to tell stories of the American West. The romance of the cowboy's life and tales about the American Indian had captured his imagination. "He didn't know about the true history and the mistreatment of the Indians," Courlander recalls. "That's what it was like in those days, for most people in the East."

And so the three children would gather close to listen, as their father's voice and words took them to faraway times and places: "Once when I was riding across the prairie, I saw a band of Indians coming after me," David would say. "I kicked my horse and galloped faster than lightning. Up ahead there was a chasm. The only way to escape was to leap across. I urged my horse forward and jumped! But on the other side, there was another band of Indians, waiting to attack!"

"What did you do, Father?" the children cried. "What did you do?"

David smiled. "I turned my horse around and went back the other way." In the kitchen, Harold's Aunt Julia would listen, a scowl on her face. She would poke her head through the door and say, "What are you talking about? *Die Leute werden über dich lachen!* People will laugh at you!" Still, she always kept one ear to the door, waiting for the next story to begin.

When he was ten years old, Harold became ill with the childhood ailments that were prevalent at the time. He was racked with coughs and often didn't have the strength to walk to school. Finally his mother sent him to one of the schools that the government had set up for children with chronic illnesses, called "open-air schools." Most of the day he spent outside, breathing in fresh air and playing vigorous games. After a year, he regained his health and returned to public school.

It was at this time that Harold began to write stories. He made up his own newspaper for the family. He created headlines, and passed out copies to his parents, aunts and uncles, sisters, and cousins—

whoever would read them. Even then, Courlander knew that his future lay in words—in stories and in writing. "By the age of ten," he said, "I'd probably outgrown my ambition to be a garbageman. . . . But I always considered myself a narrator. Even before I could articulate it, I felt I was there for that reason. If I had any endowment at all, that was it."

▲▲

BY THE TIME Harold Courlander was a teenager, the United States was stepping into a new era. Calvin Coolidge was president. The war had ended with victory for the Allies, and the League of Nations was established to try and restore peace and order to the countries of the world. In the aftermath of the war, new nations were established—among them were Austria, Hungary, and Czechoslovakia in Europe; Turkey in the Near East; and the Baltic republics of Lithuania, Latvia, and Estonia. In the United States, the 1920s came to be known as the Roaring Twenties, or the Jazz Age. The Nineteenth Amendment had given women the right to vote. Young women whose mothers and grandmothers had worn dresses down to their ankles now wore skirts above their knees and short haircuts called bobs.

Factories now produced all kinds of new domestic goods, and higher wages meant that many Americans could afford new inventions like radios, refrigerators, and Model T's. Americans wanted to forget the hardships of the war. In 1927, the first "talking picture," *The Jazz Singer,* was shown on movie screens across the country. Fans flocked by the thousands to see their sports heroes and cheered for the mighty bat of Babe Ruth in stadiums from Chicago to St. Louis to New York City. Courlander's favorite team was the Detroit Tigers, and he followed their games avidly. In those days, members

of the team would come back to their neighborhoods after a game and unofficially "coach" the young players coming up.

The 1920s also saw the growth of organized labor as the union movement gained strength in the United States. In Michigan, the Ford Motor Company was operating at peak capacity. Riding home from school on the trolley, Harold Courlander watched the workers coming home from their hours of labor out in Dearborn, the factory site. Big men, Polish and Irish, black and white, would be leaning on the straps of the car, sometimes asleep on their feet. One year, Courlander remembered, the workers of the Ford Motor Company staged a strike. Ford fought back with all the power and resources it had. Workers were beaten and kicked by hired thugs. Some were even killed. It was America, but where was the "justice for all" that his teachers had taught him about so fervently in his early days? Harold pondered these things as he went through his days of school and chores at home. He knew where his own sympathies lay—with those tired men who were struggling to keep body and spirit together, for themselves and their families, as they slept in exhaustion on the trolleys of Detroit.

▲▲

DURING HIS HIGH school years, Courlander became editor of the student newspaper. He enjoyed the job so much that he sometimes neglected his other studies. He was never in danger of failing, except for one subject, trigonometry. Courlander had a great capacity for logical thinking, but the application of sines and cosines to daily life was a mystery to him, at least the way his trigonometry teacher taught it. So when the day of the final exam came, he steeled himself for the worst. He sat down at the worn wooden desk and stared at the exam problem that lay before him. It seemed impossible. He didn't know what formulas to use. Then he looked at it again. Maybe there was another way to solve this problem? Using what he knew of regular arithmetic, he patiently set about to work out the answer. Five pages later, after scores of calculations, he arrived at the solution. And it was correct! He had solved the problem! His teacher looked at his paper skeptically. "You got the right answer," she said, "but you didn't arrive at it the way I taught you." She failed him. This was an event that Courlander remembered well into his later years. "It was the injustice of it!" he said. Still, with all the credits he had earned from his previous grades, he passed the course and graduated. Courlander spent his first semesters out of high school at Wayne State University. In 1927 he transferred to the English literature department at the University of Michigan in Ann Arbor, and a new phase of life began to open up.

In college, Harold found himself among peers whose ideas and interests were similar to his own. One of them, Betty Smith, went on to become the author of the classic novel *A Tree Grows in Brooklyn.* Quickly he made his way into the literary life of the university and became the editor of *Procession,* the student literary magazine. The magazine published poems and short stories, pieces of creative writing and fiction by the aspiring writers of the student body. But Harold had other ideas. In his studies he had learned about a professor named Guy Johnson who had studied the oral literature and languages of the black communities in the South, especially the Georgia Sea Islands. He read about Professor Johnson's linguistic theories, which presented the idea that Gullah, the islanders' language, was actually a mixture of English and African languages. Courlander was intrigued. Memories of his playground days with black friends echoed through his mind. What were the stories and songs of these

island people? He continued his research and eventually published some Sea Island poems and song lyrics in *Procession*. Student and faculty alike were appalled. "Are you out of your mind? Are you nuts? This isn't *literature!*" But Courlander stuck to his guns. In these stories and songs, he heard a beauty and poetry that was resonant and

A scene from the first production of *Swamp Mud* at the University of Michigan, 1931.

Harold Courlander with two other Hopwood Award honorees, University of Michigan, 1931.

authentic to American life and history. He continued to publish the poetry of the black South, and in 1931, drawn ever more deeply into the roots of black culture, he wrote his first play, *Swamp Mud.*

Swamp Mud tells the story of a group of black prisoners forced to work on the chain gang of a prison farm in the South. Their overseer treats them cruelly, and finally one man kills him. Still chained to two other prisoners, he escapes. In the end all three meet their death in the swamp. Esau, the oldest of the trio, is a man who finds that religious beliefs are what give him sustenance. Daniel, sentenced to life on the chain gang for a petty crime, is resigned to his circumstances. Tuesday, who killed the overseer, has his own beliefs. He rejects his oppression, and the swamp serves as a metaphor for the forces that want to "drag people down." He believes in his own stars and his own voice, and the others, not understanding him, fear him.

One of the most popular playwrights of the day was a man named Avery Hopwood. Hopwood's plays, comedies and farces, had been produced on Broadway and in regional theaters around the country. Hopwood was also an alumnus of the University of Michigan. Before his death, Hopwood wrote a large bequest to the university into his will. The money was to be used for scholarships and prizes to support new writers and creative talent. The faculty was elated. The Depression had hit the country in 1929, and any gift like this was a godsend to the college. In 1932, Harold Courlander won the Hopwood Drama Award for *Swamp Mud.* He had also won two other prizes for his plays and essays during his undergraduate years. Before he left, the head faculty of the drama department called him in for a meeting.

"You've won the Hopwood Prize," the professors said. "Now what are you going to do with it?"

Without missing a beat he replied, "I'm going east to Yale University. I want to study with George Pierce Baker, the best drama

teacher in the country." And so, with the three-hundred-dollar award in hand, a suitcase, and his typewriter, Harold Courlander took the train to New York City to begin his career as a writer and a playwright.

▲▲

COURLANDER FOUND A small room in a walk-up apartment building on 110th Street on the West Side and worked at odd jobs. When he could, he wrote book reviews for small publications. Browsing in a bookstore one day, he happened to see a title that immediately caught his eye, *The Magic Island* by a man named William Seabrook. The book was about the Caribbean island of Haiti, with descriptions of its land and of the rituals and beliefs of its people. After Courlander read the book, images of this tropical island continued to float through his head. I wonder what it's really like, he thought to himself as he walked the streets of the city or sat working at his typewriter. It was the end of August now. He knew it was time to make his plans for the year.

When he discovered that Professor Baker was out of the country, Courlander changed course. He wanted his award money to go for something truly useful, something he was really interested in doing. Once again in his head there flashed the pictures from the magic island. A Caribbean shore. Palm trees. For two days he sat and thought about his situation, but somehow he knew all the time what his decision would be. A week later, ticket in hand, he walked onto the deck of the Panama Line steamship carrying the small suitcase and typewriter. New York Harbor and the Statue of Liberty grew smaller and smaller as the boat made its way out into Lower New York Bay. The voyage had begun.

CHAPTER 2

HAITI

AFTER SEVERAL DAYS OF SAILING, the boat pulled into the harbor of Port-au-Prince. At first all Courlander could see were the mountains—tall, green mountains that hugged the coast, jutting up into the horizon. Small lights glinted and flickered around them. As they neared the dock, he saw a hum of life. All along the pier were hundreds of dock workers, the stevedores, throwing ropes out to the sides of the ships. There were no machines to haul in the vessel, only these men, their skin shining like ebony, laughing and talking as they worked together to pull in the steamship. As he stepped off the plank, Courlander heard them speaking in the musical, lilting phrases of Creole. He tipped his hat to the side in the tropical heat. Only 565 miles from the coast of Florida, the young man from the Midwest, descendant of immigrants from Central Europe, had come to a completely different world. He looked around as the movement of the crowd carried him up the dock and through customs. "It's a

Harold Courlander at the Olaffson Hotel, Port-au-Prince, 1932, on one of his first trips to Haiti. *(Courtesy Courlander Family)*

different ball game now," he said to himself. "It's up to me to learn all about it, and what the rules are here."

▲▲

THE HISTORY OF Haiti is long and complex. Its first inhabitants were the Ciboney Indians, who migrated to the Caribbean islands about two thousand years ago from Central and South America. In the third century B.C.E., they were succeeded by the Arawak peoples, also migrating from the South American continent, who established themselves throughout the Caribbean. The Taino, a subgroup of the the Arawak, became the new inhabitants of Haiti. They developed a culture of farming, fishing, and pottery. In 1492, Columbus landed on the island and named it La Isla de Española (the Island of Spain); it later became known as Hispaniola. The next wave of invasions came from Europe. First colonized by the Spaniards, and then by the French, the island was divided in two in 1697. Most of the Taino had been killed or died from diseases brought over by the Europeans. The eastern part of the island, under Spanish control, became the Dominican Republic. The western part, controlled by the French, was called Saint Domingue.

When the French colonized the island, they imported thousands of slaves from West Africa to do the work of planting and harvesting the sugar and coffee plantations. Life under slavery was brutal. In 1801, Toussaint L'Ouverture, a freed slave, led a successful revolt against the colonial masters. In 1804, under the leadership of Jean-Jacques Dessalines, the French part of the island was renamed Haiti, an Arawak word that means "land of mountains."

Haiti was the second free republic, and the only black republic, in the Western Hemisphere. The new nation had a tumultuous history,

with many changes of leaders and shifts in power. In the twentieth century, from 1915 to 1934, Haiti had come under the control of the United States. At the time that Courlander arrived, Stenio Vincent was the head of Haiti's government.

▲▲

COURLANDER GAZED AROUND at his new surroundings. His first task was to find a place to stay. After asking around in the downtown area, he heard about a pension, a small hotel, run by a German-Haitian couple called the Olaffsons. He had to traverse the main streets of Port-au-Prince to get there.

Everywhere his eyes met with new sights, sounds, and smells. The sky was a bright blue, brighter than any sky on the mainland. In the marketplace, women walked gracefully, carrying baskets of yams and fruits on their heads. Some of the large buildings were in the old French style. Shacks and smaller houses were painted in bright colors—blues, greens, yellows. A young boy showed him the way to Rue Lalue, a street near the edge of the city where the pension could be found.

From the entrance of the hotel, Courlander could look out from the porch and see the plaza and streets of Port-au-Prince. But from the window of his back room was another sight entirely. There, spread out before him, was the open countryside of Haiti, dotted with small farms and lime-covered cabins called *kay* (KAH-eeh), the homes of the *abitan* (ah-bee-TANH)—the peasants of Haiti.

"Rue Lalue was then, as now, a main route to Pétionville, but back of that street, only a few hundred yards away, was wide-open peasant countryside, covered with the gardens and *kay* of rural Haiti. Almost every night one could hear the sounds of singing and drum-

A *konbit,* or work society, hoeing land in southern Haiti. Musicians on the right play *vaksin*—bamboo trumpets—while on the left, another member carries the society's flag. *(Courtesy Courlander Estate)*

ming back there. Evening for the Haitians began at midafternoon; even when it was dark it was still evening. True night came when the barking chorus began. A distant dog would bark somewhere, and after a short silence there would be a response from another direction. From yet another direction a third dog would join the conversation. In a short while all the dogs in Port-au-Prince and its rural environs would be barking together. The chorus would be a constant backdrop for sleeping. In the morning it was the first rooster to crow that marked the beginning of day, even though it might still be dark. Other roosters joined in, and when enough of them were involved, one knew that the night was over.

"Soon there would be human sounds, women vendors calling out their wares—*figs* (bananas), *bananes* (plantains), *pistaches grillés* (roasted peanuts), *zavocats* (avocados), and so on. From the front window of the pension one could see the vendors walking with trays or baskets on their heads, or settling down by the roadside to wait for

the customers. Some had come down all the way from Pétionville, or even from more distant places."

Courlander spent his first few days exploring the city. He had planned to use the island as a place where he could concentrate on his own work, a novel or a play, perhaps. But with each passing day he was captivated more and more by the sights, sounds, and people around him. One night, early in the evening, as he sat by his window gazing at the twilight, he heard the faint sound of drumming echoing in the distance. He decided to follow the trail toward the sound. Where would it lead? Walking behind the hotel, he stepped out into the countryside and found a footpath that led him closer to the sounds of the music. Soon he came upon a small *kay.* Outside, in the yard, two drummers were playing wooden drums, carved and covered with animal skins. A woman was dancing, her head covered in a white scarf. Soon another dancer joined her. This was music for a social gathering, a family drumming party.

The musicians didn't stop the music when they saw their guest. Instead, they invited him into the circle and offered him drink and

A Saturday night *banboch,* or social dance. The drummer sits in the chair to the far right. *(Courtesy Courlander Estate)*

food. Courlander stayed and listened to the singing. At midnight, he made his way down the trail. For the next few days, he followed the sound of music whenever he heard it, and in Haiti in 1932, that was very often indeed. Almost every day he saw people singing songs even as they worked in the fields, or gathering to hear the drummers play for rituals and ceremonies.

People were friendly, and with the few words of Creole that he was able to pick up, Courlander sensed that stories were being told around him all the time. If only he could understand them! Up in the mountains he went, and slowly he began to get a picture of the life of the farmers and musicians he was meeting. In his first book on Haiti, *Haiti Singing,* he described what he was beginning to see and understand:

> In the hills of Haiti everyone sings and dances. Babies of three years dance Vodoun and Pétro with their elders. Boys of seven are already master drummers under the teaching of their fathers, who learned from their own fathers. And old women weighed down by years and infirmities still dance *Ibo* with their shoulders.
>
> In Haiti everyone works. If they do not work they do not live. Most of them work very hard. But whether they work hard or not so hard, living is difficult and unbounteous. Women walk great distances with heavy loads on their heads; some of them walk all day and night to get to market, where they may earn eighty cents on their Congo beans and cotton, and then they walk all day and all night to get home. And the men plant and till their gardens with a machete or a hoe, hang their maize and karrif corn high in the branches of a tree to dry. . . . They are patient of a summer sun which bakes the ground hard and unfruitful, of earth which sometimes yields not enough to keep their bodies living. But when it is time to dance and sing, nature pours forth spiritual riches from the large end of the horn.

Dancers salute the *lwa* (l-wah), or deities, in a Vodoun ceremony. The *ougan* (oo-gahn) priest stands at the far left holding the *ason* (ah-sohn), the sacred rattle. *(Courtesy Courlander Estate)*

As the days passed, Courlander began to realize there were two very different types of Haitian people. There were the well-to-do business types and politicians, who lived in the grand houses and sent their children to universities in New York, Philadelphia, and Paris. But the people who drew his interest were the *abitan,* the country people, the so-called lower classes. These were the people who, very often, had never attended school, or if they did, it was only for a short time in their early years. They did not speak classical French (the official language of Haiti, taught in the schools) but the rich mélange of French and African languages called Creole. They lived on the land and from the land. Their work, their play, their solitude, and their social gatherings were all connected to the cycles of planting, harvesting, and plowing the rugged soil of the Haitian mountainside.

Courlander began to make new friends. Many of them were the pension workers, who had left their farming villages to come to work in Port-au-Prince. One of his best friends was a man named Libera Bordereaux. Libera was from the south of Haiti. His father had been a respected priest of Vodoun. Vodoun is the name of the religion practiced for generations in Haiti. *Vodoun* means "spirit" or "deity" in the Fon language of the West African country of Dahomey (now called Benin). During the sixteenth, seventeenth and eighteenth centuries, slaves were captured and sold to European traders from all over Africa. Packed together in chains on small wooden boats, they were brought to the islands of the New World. The captives all spoke their different languages and had their own highly developed belief systems, whether they were Akan, Yoruba, Fon, Ibo, or Hausa.

Living together under slavery forced these peoples from different regions and cultures to learn to communicate with one another. Gradually, over generations, they created a new religion that combined many of their tribes' gods and spirits with elements of Christianity. Because many of the slaves brought to Haiti had come from Dahomey, it became a major influence on the Haitian belief system and way of life. There was even a saying in the countryside: "Haiti is the child of Dahomey."

As Courlander listened to the people around him, he heard many such references to Africa—in daily speech, in music, in proverbs and stories. This began to intrigue him more and more. So much of African civilization had survived on this New World island. How was it possible? He wanted to discover more, to see if he could uncover the roots of this "old-yet-new" culture and way of life.

Once Libera knew that Courlander was interested in these things, he invited him to many ceremonies and gatherings. Libera himself

Libera Bordereaux, who helped Courlander with his research during Courlander's many trips to Haiti. *(Courtesy Courlander Estate)*

was from a town in the south of Haiti called Léogâne. In this remote area, African rituals had been practiced for many generations. One day, he brought Courlander to see his family. When they arrived, a ceremony was about to take place. They welcomed Libera joyfully, for they hadn't seen him in two years. As his grandmother danced, she hugged him, and several of the other women waved flags and sang. Courlander, too, was welcomed. At this ceremony, the family wanted to speak to ancestors who had passed away long ago—"*lemò anba dlo*" (the spirits who live below the sea). Only the *ougan* (oo-gahn), the priest, had the skills and knowledge to communicate with them. With Libera and his family and friends, Courlander entered the ceremonial house, the *oufò* (oo-faw), or Vodoun temple. On the floor, the priest had drawn *vèvè* (veh-VEH)—intricate patterns that represented signs of the Vodoun deities who would be invited to the ceremony. A tall column called a peristyle stood in the center of the

A *vèvè,* or ritual design, made from corn flour is drawn as part of a Vodoun ceremony to honor a deity. This is the *vèvè* for the deity Simbi. *(Courtesy Courlander Estate)*

space. Much of the music and dance took place around this peristyle. Courlander later described the event in *Haiti Singing.*

The drummers sat in their places. In Haitian religious music, drumming is all-important. Usually three drums are played: the *maman,* the *segon,* and the *boula,* the smallest drum. Another musician plays the iron bells to help keep time. As Courlander was to learn, each rhythm belonged to a different family of deities. When the drummers play and sing strongly enough and well enough, the spirit of a deity "enters" one of the dancers, and what is called possession, or trance, takes place. This happened that night in Léogâne. As the music and singing continued, one of the dancers began to tremble. She began to twist and turn. The deity who had entered her was a strong male spirit called Chebo. Possessed by Chebo, the woman lifted up a chicken. After she danced for several minutes, the chicken was sacrificed as an offering to the spirit. The strength of Chebo within her, the woman picked up a machete. She danced and twirled. From her lips came a strange language, neither French nor Creole nor even African.

It was a special language, the language of the gods.

Soon after, the woman was led to a room where she could rest. The world of the *lwa,* the ancestor deities, had come to Léogâne. Then the priest carried out a basket. His servants placed it on a small wooden table covered with a white cloth. In this basket were the symbolic objects that would help him communicate with the ancestral spirits. As Courlander watched, the priest lit a candle. He closed his eyes and began to communicate with the spirits, intoning in a special language. Through his voice, the people gathered in the *oufò* heard the words of the deity Papa Loko, who greeted them in Creole:

"Bonjou moun mwen yo, se Papa Loko!" (Good day, my people. It is I, Papa Loko.)

Musicians playing for a ceremony in northern Haiti. The boy on the left, who is twelve or thirteen years old, is skilled enough to accompany the lead drummer. *(Courtesy Courlander Estate)*

"*Bonjou, chè papa!*" (Good day, dear father!) the people answered.

After greeting the participants, Papa Loko's voice faded away. Courlander heard the *ougan*'s voice again, but this time it sounded completely different. He was speaking in the voice of an old woman. Family members recognized her as Moyise, who had died several years before. She was crying and asking after her children and grandchildren. One by one, voices of the ancestors spoke through the *ougan,* and the people talked with them. Another ancestor spirit, whose name was Docile, asked that her grave be moved, as she had been buried next to a thief. The farmer Alixe, her relation, who stood by the *ougan,* listened and told her that he would take care of it. Satisfied, her voice, too, faded away. Courlander

listened. At least twenty different spirits conversed with the people through the *ougan*. The service ended just as the light of dawn began to glimmer in the sky.

When they returned to Port-au-Prince, Courlander asked his friend many questions. What did the songs mean? What was the significance of the *vèvè* designs? Why did the women wave flags? Why did the drummers play a certain rhythm he had heard? How did it come about that some people became *lwa*—ancestors—and others did not? Libera shared with him all he knew of the answers to these questions.

Courlander recalled, "If Libera was with me, when a woman went into one of these possessions, I learned it was really more than that. He'd say that her body was taken over by one of the deities. And she was doing all kinds of funny things (as it seemed to me)—motions of various kinds, dance steps, jumping on a burning fire. So I'd ask him what it all meant, and he'd say, 'Her head is being inhabited by such and such a deity, and she's doing these things to demonstrate the qualities or the personality of the deity.' The next morning he'd come in and would go into great detail about these deities and so forth and so on. This went on through all my visits to Haiti until my second to last visit some years ago."

▲▲

COURLANDER'S FIRST TRIP to Haiti lasted six months. He didn't write the novel he had planned. Instead, he spent almost all of his time talking to people and taking trips into the mountains. All the while he was listening to the songs and the stories that people would tell to one another. In his room he began to jot down notes—a song here, a story there. By listening to the lyrics and asking his friends what

they meant, he began to learn more and more of the Creole language. "I began to get explanations and then explanations of explanations. I was beginning to pick up a little of the language. It crossed my mind to put down on paper some of the things I was hearing. I wasn't too clear why I was doing it, but that was all part of learning the language, too. I was beginning to put songs down and the words, the lyrics."

Courlander's interest was not centered solely on the rituals and music. He was also touched by and drawn to the character and quality of the people around him. As he was walking through the streets one day, he saw an old man begging for a few coins to feed his family. Courlander reached into his pocket. All he had was a five-dollar bill. He said to the man, "I'd like to give you some coins, but all I have is this paper money." The old man said, "If you wait here, I will come back and bring you the change." Courlander did not hesitate. He gave the old man the paper money. The old man walked down the street slowly, because of his age. But Courlander was patient. He knew the old man would return. And after some time, he saw him walking back slowly, and he had the exact amount of change in his hand. Such was the honesty and dignity Courlander encountered again and again in the people he met on the island.

Ever eager for soaking up narrative, Courlander was surrounded by storytellers. For in Haiti, everyone is considered a potential storyteller. Once he heard Libera talk about a friend of his who had been cheated at the marketplace. Libera laughed. *"O, li te yon gwo Bouki!"* (He was just like *Bouki!*)

"Bouki," Courlander said, "who is this Bouki I've heard so much about?" So Libera told him a story much like this one, "Bouki and Ti Malice Go Fishing," which appears in *The Drum and the Hoe: Life and Lore of the Haitian People.*

Cric! Crac!

Bouki and Ti Malice went into the fishing business together. Ti Malice painted the name St. Jacques on the front of the boat, poured some rum over it, and christened it. Bouki took some rum and poured it over the back end of the boat and christened it Papa Pierre. They went out to sea and caught fish. When they came home, Ti Malice counted the fish. "There are eighteen fish," he said. "How shall we divide them?"

"I'll take one and you take one until they're gone," Bouki said.

Malice said: "There are so few fish it isn't worthwhile. You take all the fish today and I'll take all the fish tomorrow."

"Oh no," Bouki said, "I'm not totally stupid. You take all today and I'll take them all tomorrow." So Malice took all the fish.

The went out again the next day, and when they came home Malice counted again and said, "There are so few, you take all today and I'll take all tomorrow."

"Oh no," Bouki said, "you're trying to cheat me. You take all today and I'll take all tomorrow." So Malice took all.

The next day they went out again. And when they were returning Ti Malice said, "Waille, such a small catch. I'm glad it's your turn to take all today."

Bouki became angry and said, "Are you trying to break my head? I'm no fool. You take the catch today and I'll take it tomorrow."

Every day Ti Malice took the whole catch. Every day Bouki got nothing. Malice got fatter and fatter and Bouki got thinner. Every day it was this way, until one day Bouki looked at Ti Malice and saw how fat he was getting. It came to him suddenly that he had been cheated. He shouted at Ti Malice and began to chase him. They ran through the peristyle of the town hounfor *and Ti Malice said "cata-cata," imitating the sound of a drum, and called on Ogoun and Damballa to save him.*

They ran through the church, where the priest was holding a service. Malice crossed himself and said a quick prayer, without stopping for a second, and

ran out again. They ran, ran, ran, and Bouki was getting closer. Ti Malice came to a limekiln with a hole in it. He tried to crawl through, but he got stuck at the hips. No matter how hard he tried, he couldn't get through. Finally Bouki came along. He stopped and looked in all directions. There was no Ti Malice, only the behind facing him from the limekiln.

Bouki put on his best manners, and said, "Behind, have you seen Ti Malice?"

The behind replied, "Take off your hat when you address me."

Bouki took off his hat to Ti Malice's behind. He said politely, "Why are you smiling at me? I only asked if you saw Ti Malice?"

"I smile when I please," the behind said.

"Have you seen Ti Malice?" Bouki said.

"Push me and I'll tell you," the behind said.

Bouki pushed.

"Harder," the behind said.

Bouki pushed harder.

"Harder yet," the behind said.

Bouki gave a big push, and Ti Malice went through the hole into the limekiln. And that was the way he made his escape.

Courlander soon learned that Bouki and Ti Malice are a pair—two of the best-known characters in Haitian folklore. In almost every story, Bouki is the dupe, the fool, while Ti Malice, ever clever, is always ready to take advantage of him.

Although Libera had a great deal of knowledge about Vodoun, he himself did not practice it anymore. One day Courlander was speaking to him, and found out the reason why: "You see," said Libera, "my wife's family is Protestant. Till now she has not been able to bear a child. My wife's parents think that it is because of Vodoun that she cannot bear a child. They say I must give it up forever. Only then will she be able to have a child." Courlander nodded. He

understood his friend. Libera was a man of honor who would do anything necessary to have peace in the family. But he also thought, How strange, for here it is the Protestants who are superstitious. They objected to Vodoun because it is full of superstition, but they have superstitious beliefs about Vodoun!

One evening, while Courlander was sitting in his room at the Olafssons', he heard a knock on his door. It was Libera. He was very concerned. His wife was quite sick. She was in great pain and had sent Libera to find Courlander. "I've had a dream," she told her husband. "Only he can cure me!" Courlander was shaken. He understood the power of dreams, but he also knew that he was no doctor. He told Libera that he would find the nearest doctor in Port-au-Prince to help his wife. He went in search, but the doctor wasn't at home. When he returned to the hotel, Libera begged again, "Please, my friend. My wife believes in you. We have no doctors in the countryside. You are our only hope."

So, worried about what he was going to do, Courlander walked with his friend to the small lime-covered cabin. Libera's wife was lying on a mat on the floor, writhing in pain. She told Courlander that the pain was in her head and her ears. He examined her as best he could and deduced from the symptoms that she was suffering from an abscess. Of course, he knew that a true doctor would know just what to do with an abscess. It would probably be a very simple procedure to drain and clean the area. But as Courlander put it, "That was not my ball park!" But he did remember how many times when he was young his father had cured his ailments—from earaches to stomachaches to muscle sprains—with salt. His father would heat salt up in a frying pan, wrap it up with a cloth, and apply it to whatever area was in pain.

Well, Courlander thought to himself, it certainly won't make it worse, and maybe it will make it better. He told Libera to find some

salt, while he stayed in the house with his wife. Libera ran off and, in due time, came back with a bag of salt he had borrowed from a neighbor. Courlander heated the salt over the stove, just as his father had done, and then wrapped it in a piece of cloth and put it on the side of Madame Libera's head. When it cooled, he heated up the salt again. After a while he turned to Libera.

"There, my friend. This is what you must do. Continue to apply the heat with the cloth and see if that helps." Then he made his way back to the hotel.

The next day, as he sat over his morning coffee, he saw Libera coming toward him. Uh-oh, he said to himself. I'd better go fetch the doctor! But as Libera approached, he saw a big smile on his face. "You see, my wife was right about you. She is cured!" Courlander was happy, and silently thanked his father for the knowledge he had given him.

"But Libera," he said to his friend, "don't tell anyone you know about it, or all the people from the countryside will be coming to the Olaffsons', asking me to cure them!" Libera agreed. His secret was safe.

▲▲

COURLANDER WENT BACK to New York. But he knew that he wanted to return to Haiti as soon as he could. Now he wanted to begin to collect the stories and songs of the *abitan* in earnest. If he could write down and publish all the things he had been learning, it would mean that more people on the outside would begin to understand what he was beginning to see from being closer to the inside: the life and values of Haitian people.

But it would be a number of years before he could fulfill his plans. Soon after he returned to New York, an urgent communication

came to him from Detroit. Harold spoke to his sister Adelaide. "Harold," she told him, "we can't make ends meet here in the city. Father can't make any money from his business. My husband is an attorney, but who can pay for lawyers these days? We've decided to leave the city. We're going to try and beat the Depression another way. We've got enough money, if we pool our resources, to buy some land up in Romeo, in central Michigan. We're going to try to farm, but we need your help. We can't do it on our own."

Courlander looked at the lights of the city. He looked at the notes he had gathered and the reel-to-reel recordings he had started to collect of the drumming and songs he had listened to in Haiti. He knew that it was time to say good-bye to all of this for now. He had to help his family.

CHAPTER 3

THE FARM

HAROLD'S MOTHER, TILLIE, died in 1932. She had been ill for some time with "consumption" (tuberculosis) and had spent her last years in a sanitarium in Colorado. Coping with her long illness and death had taken its toll on everyone in the family, but especially on David Courlander. Still, he had the energy to move to a new home with Harold, Adelaide, her husband, Sam Frane, and their four children, Lenore, Alan, Bob, and Joan, who were then ten, eight, four, and one, respectively. Looking back, Courlander said, "We learned the hard way about farming and sometimes wondered if the farm was supporting us or we were supporting the farm."

Most of their new neighbors had lived in Romeo for years and were accustomed to the land and the farming life. The Courlanders had to learn from scratch. They had a barn, where they raised cows and chickens. They had a few horses to graze and to help with the plowing. They planted squash, beans, and tomatoes in their garden

and used the acreage of fields for potatoes and corn, their only cash crops.

Courlander had spent many months in the mountains of Haiti watching the men work in their *konbit*, or work teams. He had seen the men hoeing, working from dawn until dusk, sometimes in bare feet, walking, bending, plowing, and harvesting in the fields. He had seen the women, too, hard at work in the gardens, or winnowing grains in large straw baskets. He had gone to the University of Michigan and had lived in New York City. He had written a play and had published a few short stories. But now, he himself was trying to survive with the rest of America. Now he had become the farmer.

Years later Courlander said, "The farming years, they built my self-esteem the way nothing else could. You had to do everything. If your car broke down, there was no service station around the corner. The tractor, you had to take care of it. Nobody could do these things like in the city here—no drugstore around the corner. . . . If it was going to rain and you had hay, it had to come in from the field; it's two o'clock in the morning, you had to get up in the middle of the night and go out, hitch the team and go out with the wagon and bring the hay in at two o'clock in the morning. The responsibility was totally on us, this is what I learned."

In Haiti, everyone had a special role to play on the farm. Men worked, women worked, fufilling their roles so that the whole community could survive. There was even a Haitian proverb: "*Tanbouye pa kapab danse*" (The drummer doesn't dance). Each person has to stick to his or her role. On the Courlander farm, there was a job for everyone, too. David Courlander was in charge of the chickens. Somehow, chickens were something he knew a lot about. He had even kept some in the family's backyard in Detroit. So everyone in

the family knew to let him buy the chickens they would need for eggs. He kept them in the chicken coop that he built himself. After a while, he got to know the chickens so well, he gave each of them a name. One day, after a bout of drought and bad weather, Adelaide said to her father: "Dad, you better kill a chicken for dinner today. This is Sunday." It was like somebody had slapped his face. He said, "Kill a chicken? They're all egg producers. Kill a chicken?" Adelaide looked down at the floor. "Yes, we need it for dinner." Her father grew pale. He went out the door and disappeared; nobody knew where he was. "He refused to kill a chicken, just by being absent, somebody else had to do that. He knew every chicken."

The Depression went on, and so did life at the farm. Sometimes Courlander would work in the fields, plowing till sunset. Sometimes there wasn't enough money to buy a new pair of shoes, so he would often have to work barefoot. As he stood in the fields at twilight, he would see the sunlit island in his mind's eye: Libera laughing at a funny story, Mr. and Mrs. Olafsson setting out cups of fragrant coffee in the morning, the sound of drums and children's laughter as they played a game, passing a stone from one to the other and singing:

Jésus, Marie, Joseph, oh
Rat là mangé pigeon moin
Jésus, Marie, Joseph, oh
Rat là mangé pigeon moin
Rat passé, Robinette passé
Fai' ti Marie marché, allé là . . .

(Jesus, Mary, Joseph, oh
The rat has eaten my pigeon
Jesus, Mary, Joseph, oh

The rat has eaten my pigeon
The rat goes by, Robinette goes by
Make little Mary walk, go there . . .)

Then he had to shake his head. Someday he would return, and somehow he knew he had to keep writing.

He had his typewriter, but he needed a quiet place, with no distractions, if he was to get anything done. He tried to use a tent, which he set up near the house. It didn't work very well as a writing place, and one night somebody came along and stole it, so the problem remained. Sometime later, he was able to find a solution from an unexpected source.

▲▲

IN 1936, A DROUGHT hit central Michigan. Every day, Alan or young Bob would check the sky for a sign of a cloud, a drop of rain. But the sky was a bright, hard blue. Then one day a small black cloud appeared on the horizon. At first, no one paid any attention to it. It seemed so small and distant. The cloud grew closer, bigger. Within minutes, it seemed, the sky turned black, the birds fell silent.

"My nephew Alan and I started down the lane," Courlander later wrote, "and were just passing the orchard when the wind hit. An empty barrel bounded across the lane just ahead of us, struck a large rock, and shattered, the individual staves riding away on the wind. Apples came like shrapnel from the orchard, some bounding, some traveling horizontally. Though the daylight was rapidly fading, we could still see a short distance ahead, where more debris was blowing onto our path—fence rails, tree limbs, and boards from our lumber pile. It became impossible to go forward. Holding hands, Alan

and I turned back and passed around the lee side of the barn just in time to see a large piece of the barn roof rise up and float over our heads, twisting and turning until it came down in our prize cornfield.

"On the other side of the barn we were again in the fury of the wind. Hail and rain began to fall, though in truth not so much falling as travelling horizontally. The short distance to the house seemed very far. I myself do not recall it, but my sister said later that Alan and I were crawling on all fours when we reached the door. When we got inside someone was just lighting an oil lamp, the electric power having gone off. The family was gathered in the kitchen, all except my father and young Bob. They said my father and Bob were out in the barn. The barn? It was coming apart and there was nothing to do but go after them. I could not open the barn door because of the pressure of the wind, and so I banged on it and shouted until it opened a couple of inches and I saw my father's face. I motioned to him come out. He shook his head and I faintly heard him yell, 'Do you think I'm crazy?' Finally I persuaded him and he came out with Bob. The three of us somehow made it back to the safety of the house, though how safe it was we really did not know.

"By this time it was totally black outside. All we could hear were the roar of wind and various kinds of debris striking the house. . . . At some point [my sister] began to wonder about how things were faring upstairs, and she sent Bob up to make sure all the windows were closed. When he came down she asked, 'Are they closed?' He said calmly, 'Yes, they're all closed,' then added seemingly as an afterthought, 'but I think the roof is off. Water is coming through the ceiling.'

"As suddenly as it had appeared, the storm passed over and the sun came out. Later we heard that a hundred-and-ten-mile wind had cut

a wide swath all the way to Lake St. Clair and that ten inches of rain had fallen in forty-five minutes. But those are only statistics, which do not have any feeling in them. Better remembered are the sights we saw outside when the event was over."

Fortunately, no one in the family had been hurt, but their land and livestock were another matter. Miraculously, their herd of cows had stayed together, swimming through the rising waters until they reached high ground on the hilltop. But all of their white leghorn chickens, the prize possessions of David Courlander, had disappeared, the chicken coops turned upside down. The corn crop, too, had been devastated, the ears hanging limply on their stalks. Farther off in the woods, strong trees had been lifted and uprooted completely.

Courlander surveyed the damage. They had much work to do to put the farm back to rights again, but meanwhile, the fallen trees gave him an idea. Maybe this was a way to get a place to write—maybe he could build himself a log cabin. With the help of a neighbor, he dragged the logs off to the saw mill. Later, after they had split them, Courlander built a stone foundation. With his nephew Alan he set up a four-by-four framework, and with the remaining stones, he built a fireplace. Little by little, dragging, pounding, with cement blocks to set the floor and mortar to fill in the cracks between the logs, the cabin was built. Now he had a place to write. He even drilled his own well. In the evenings he would cook over the stone fireplace, and in the mornings heat up coffee. Raccoons, possums, and field mice often stopped by to visit, as well as neighbors, his niece and nephews, and their farm dog. Abraham Lincoln had been a childhood hero of Harold Courlander's. Now he too had split logs and read by the light of candle!

Like his father, Courlander developed personal relationships with the animals of the farm. He especially loved the cows. They seemed

Courlander's log cabin in Romeo, Michigan, was built from trees felled in a storm. *(Photo: Harold Courlander)*

to have personalities of their own. One day, he had to go do some work on the far side of the pasture. As he set off, one of the calves broke off from the herd and began to follow him. She ran playfully back and forth as he walked over the fields. By and by he had to cross a stream by way of a narrow wooden bridge. The calf ran up behind him and butted him into the river! Then she turned and trotted back to the herd, and for all Courlander could see, she was laughing to herself. One day, some of the cows had to be sent off by train to the cattle yard for slaughter. That was the day that he realized he could never be a true farmer. It hurt too much.

Courlander was beginning to take some satisfaction in his growing independence and knowledge of farming ways. He was particularly proud of his ability to drive a tractor and his control of the machine over all kinds of terrain. While he was working alone at the far edge of their fields one day, the tractor took a bad turn and fell over sideways. He jumped out just in time, for he might have been crushed. But now it was a matter of pride. He didn't want to go back and get help; he had to get that tractor up by himself. All day he worked with a piece of wood, using it as a lever to push the tractor back up on its wheels. Finally he set it to rights again and drove home, sobered by his accident and near brush with death.

▲▲

FROM 1933 TO 1938, Courlander worked on the farm. (Toward the end of those years, he began again to make visits to New York City.) In 1932, Franklin Delano Roosevelt had been elected president, with his promise of a "new deal for the American people." Despite many obstacles, the Roosevelt administration was giving new hope to thousands, as the federal government spearheaded programs such as the WPA (the Works Projects Administration) and the CCC (Civilian Conservation Corps) to create more jobs and stimulate the economy. Finally, conditions for the family improved. Sam, Courlander's brother-in-law, had kept enough of his business going so that he could return to his work as an attorney. Adelaide and the children were ready to get back to city life. The children had complained bitterly about their life in Romeo, but for Courlander, hard though it was, it had also been a wonderful time: a time of learning, of self-reliance, and of taking care of those who were near to him. The memories of the farm would stay with him for years afterward,

coloring his view of people, work, and the reality of the human being's capacity to survive and endure.

But his plans had always entailed going back to New York, and to the Caribbean. He needed to build up his finances and so he stayed for some time in Detroit, picking up freelance writing jobs. It was at that time that he met the woman who would become his first wife, Ella Schneideman, a social worker. Together they planned to move back to New York, where he could continue to pursue his research and she her own career.

CHAPTER 4

NEW YORK AND THE CARIBBEAN

THE DEPRESSION WAS NOT THE ONLY great event shaping the decade of the 1930s. Throughout Europe, in the aftermath of World War I, political changes and economic conditions were giving rise to the ominous forces of Fascism in Italy, and to the National Socialist Party—the Nazi regime—in Germany. Mussolini and the Italian army invaded Ethiopia in 1935. In 1936, General Francisco Franco and his followers staged a revolt that led to civil war and the victory of his Fascist regime in Spain. Josef Stalin ruled the peoples of the Soviet Union with an iron hand. In that same year, Hitler was gathering troops in the Rhineland, on the border of France, while France and England did little to stop him. Once again, history was transforming Courlander's world and shaping the direction of his life.

Closer to home, there were some ominous developments in the Caribbean, too. In 1930, Rafael Trujillo, an army general, took con-

trol of the government of the Dominican Republic. At that time, many Haitians had crossed the western border of their country to find work on the sugar plantations and farmlands of the Dominican Republic. They were tolerated by the Dominicans because they afforded a source of cheap labor for the back-breaking work of cane cutting.

Over the previous hundred years, there had been much animosity between the two countries. Trujillo resented the intrusion of so many Haitians on his land. On October 2, 1937, Trujillo secretly gave orders to his army to "eliminate" the Haitians living on the borders within the Dominican Republic. In a matter of three days, thousands of Haitian families—men, women, and children—were rounded up by Trujillo's soldiers and slaughtered with brutal efficiency. Many were drowned or decapitated. Their houses were burned. The streams and rivers of the Massacre Highlands (ironically, the name for this area) were flowing with the blood of innocent people. It took days for the news to leak out, and when it became known, even Trujillo's supporters, both in the United States and the Dominican Republic, were horrified. Courlander was visiting New York City at the time. One day, he received a letter from a friend of his, a priest. As he read the letter, tears began to stream down his face. Could this be true? Soon after, he set sail for Haiti. When he arrived, he traveled to the Dominican border and spoke to people there, refugees from the massacre. Everything the priest had told him was true. Although he hadn't witnessed it personally, the stories he heard and the faces of the people told him everything. A terrible injustice had taken place.

Trujillo had now become part of the folklore of the Haitian people. They called him "Tue-jillo" (Killer of Innocents). Courlander was aware, too, of another motivation for Trujillo's atrocities. In

addition to the hostility bred from historical circumstances, Trujillo also had a great fear and resentment of people of African descent, even though his own grandmother was herself Haitian! Trujillo wanted a country that looked to the world like a European nation, not an African one, despite the fact that many Dominicans were themselves of mixed or purely African descent. Anger at the racism, the abuse, and the injustice boiled within Courlander. What could he do? He was not a soldier or a politician. But he was a writer. The world might be silent, but he would not be.

Courlander returned to New York. He reported the massacre in a news piece for the *New Republic* in November 1937. He also began work on what was to be his first novel, *The Caballero.* Using thinly disguised names for the island and the characters, Courlander began to draw his picture of the dictator. Always a meticulous researcher, he decided that he should go directly to the source for his material, so he wrote a letter to Trujillo himself. "Dear General, I am writing a book about you. Do you have any information that would be

The cover of Courlander's first novel, *The Caballero.* Published in 1940, the book details the rise and fall of a Caribbean dictator much like General Rafael Trujillo of the Dominican Republic. (*Courtesy Courlander Estate*)

helpful to my work? I will send you a copy when it is completed." And Trujillo, always seeking to broadcast the glory of his name, sent him books and pamphlets that described him in only the highest, most admiring terms. They were useless, Courlander said later, except for helping him to see with even greater clarity Trujillo's true character. Every day, Courlander researched and then wrote, letting his imagination play out the history of his characters. He wrote feverishly, spurred on by his knowledge of the horrors that had occurred:

> Without warning a contingent of guardias arrive from Guanabana [Dominican Republic] in army trucks. . . . The M'bassans [Haitians] stand frightened and fixed where they are. Women begin to understand, and run after their children. A boy slips out and races like mad for the cane field, where his father works. Some of the women try to get out too, but the guardias cut them off. . . . The people of the compound are hysterical, the women shrieking in terror, the men throwing rocks. Already there are half a dozen bodies lying in open view. Everything is nightmare, guardias running after their kill. Now the workers begin to arrive from the cane fields, machetes in hand. They become the targets, while the women and children run desperately toward the hills.

During this tumultuous time, many artists were caught up with the progressive movement. The effects of the Depression, and the rise of fascism in Europe, gave impetus to their concerns for economic rights and social justice for all Americans. Black writers and poets such as Langston Hughes, Gwendolyn Brooks, and Richard Wright were emerging with their own powerful voices to speak of their people's struggles and triumphs. Courlander, too, was part of this world and contributed his own voice to it.

The Federal Theater was one of the projects that grew out of the Roosevelt era's Works Progress Administration. Writers, actors, and directors from all over the country were involved, creating new plays and recasting classic repertoire from a contemporary perspective. In New York City, under the directorship of John Houseman and Orson Welles, the Federal Theater had a branch in Harlem, and they were always looking for new material for the company.

Courlander presented Houseman with the script of *Swamp Mud*. Houseman liked it very much and, in 1940, it was produced as a one-act play. It was during this time of literary and cultural activity that Courlander came to know Langston Hughes. He and Courlander were to remain friends for many years, corresponding about their work and lives.

The New York of the late 1930s and early '40s was full of writers, artists, and poets practicing their craft. Courlander and his wife, Ella, settled in Greenwich Village in Manhattan, on Carmine Street. Although he was writing alone in his apartment, Courlander felt that he was part of a community of fellow struggling artists. Not every writer was or became famous, but many had distinctive characters and personalities. Courlander remembered one man in the Village, a bohemian named Joe Gould, who claimed he was working on an "oral history of the world." Poets would read their work in small restaurants in exchange for a meal or a place to sleep. Joe was known for walking into the local automat (automated cafeteria) and making sandwiches out of leftover bread and ketchup. Once, while Courlander was sitting at a table, Joe Gould walked in, and someone called out, "Get out the ketchup! Here comes Joe Gould!"

Painters would display their work every year in the spring art shows in Washington Square. One day Courlander was walking with

Ella and they stopped in front of some sketches drawn by two young boys, brothers probably, who looked to be about ten and eight years old. A woman stopped and admired one of their sketches. "How much is that?" she asked the older boy. "Ten cents," he replied. She paid him for the sketch, and the ten-year-old said to his little brother, "Quick! Go home and make another one!" Art in Greenwich Village took many shapes and forms!

In order to finish his novel, Courlander realized he needed to spend more time in Haiti. He completed *The Caballero* there and it was published in 1940. In a letter to a friend he wrote: "Reviews were good but buyers were scarce." Faithful to his word, he sent a copy to Trujillo. He did not hear anything back from the dictator, but some months later, Courlander traveled to Havana, Cuba. He was planning to record Afro-Cuban music there and compare it to the music and dances of Haiti. One day, he passed by a bookstore. Curious about the fate of his novel, he asked the bookstore owner if he had ever heard of a book called *The Caballero.*

"Oh, yes," the bookstore owner said. "We had many copies here when it was first published."

"And what happened to them?" said Courlander. "I don't see any here now."

"The first week they were in the store, two very well dressed gentlemen with sunglasses came in and asked for the book. They bought up every copy. They bought up every copy of the book in Havana. You can't find them now." Of course, Courlander knew who those well-dressed gentlemen were. They were "messengers" of Trujillo. Clearly the general did not want the book and its portrayal of him to be read by anyone, and so he had confiscated all the copies. Still Courlander smiled to himself: "If that happened in New York, I'd have a best-seller on my hands!"

▲▲

BY THE END of the 1930s Courlander, continuing his documentation work in Haiti, had collected enough material to write an in-depth study. At about that time, he came into contact with Melville Herskovits, who was one of the leading anthropologists in African and African Diaspora cultures. The two became friends and colleagues. With Herskovits's help, Courlander was able to find a publisher for his first book on the island, *Haiti Singing.* The book was well received, noted in reviews for its descriptions of instruments and its extensive song collection.

Frontispiece and title page for *Haiti Singing,* published in 1940. Many of the instruments identified here also appear in photographs and on later recordings such as the three-volume set for Folkways, *Music of Haiti.* (*Courtesy Courlander Estate*)

In 1940, Courlander decided he would like to go to Cuba to research and record. Following his interest in African-derived music, he wanted to see if there were connections in other parts of the Caribbean as well. Funding from a small grant allowed him to make the trip. What he saw and heard in Cuba fascinated him. With help from friends and a renowned music scholar, Fernando Ortiz, he was able to record the music and songs of Afro-Cuban cults. Many of these cults were outlawed by the government, but through his connections, Courlander was able to gain access to them. As in Haiti, each cult had preserved not only the drum rhythms but also the African language of its origins. The trip to Cuba, although not as long or intensive as his work in Haiti, did help to confirm his ideas about Africans in the Americas. A whole civilization that had been brutally uprooted had reformed and was persisting, creating its own dynamic traditions and art forms.

Years later, when he had a chance to visit Africa and meet African musicians, Courlander was to see confirmation of the African connections he had been pursuing. One day he played one of the rhythms he had learned in Haiti for a Nigerian, a man of the Ibo people. The man looked at Courlander with tears in his eyes. "You are playing my music. That is the music of my village, my people!" What Courlander was discovering in the 1940s was that music was a powerful force, powerful enough, when carried on by the people, to preserve the very essence of a civilization and pass it on to the next generation with remarkable purity and authenticity.

In New York, Courlander made friends with a Haitian musician, Wilfred Beauchamps. He often recorded Beauchamps and practiced the drumming patterns he had learned in Haiti with him. Courlander was not a trained musician, but he had a fine musical ear and an innate affinity for rhythms and percussion. On a few occasions,

Musicians from the Afro-Cuban Yoruba tradition called *Lucumí* play the ritual *batá* drums during Courlander's field trip to Cuba in 1940. *(Photo: Harold Courlander. Courtesy the Center for Folklife Programs and Cultural Studies, Smithsonian Institution)*

Haitian or African drummers came to him to check if their drumming beats were the correct ones! One of them, Alphonse Cimber, became a well-known performer who played in stage and film productions. Courlander's books, articles, and recordings were beginning to form a body of important material. Slowly, scholars and others began to refer to his work when they wanted to learn more or had questions themselves about the roots of these cultural expressions. But there was always more to do, and much more to learn.

CHAPTER 5

ETHIOPIA AND WORLD WAR II

BY 1942 THE UNITED STATES was fully engaged in World War II. Young Americans were fighting on all fronts in Europe, North Africa, and the Pacific. When it was his turn to be called and Harold Courlander went to the draft board, the officer in charge asked him what he could do. "Well, I'm a writer," said Courlander. "And I've done a lot of research and recording." The draft officer looked at him. "We'll find something for you to do."

At that time, German submarines were cruising just outside the boundary line of American waters. All troop movements had to be kept secret. Courlander was assigned to join a fleet that was crossing the Atlantic. Although their official destination was unknown, Courlander suspected they were on the way to North Africa. He tells the story of the journey: "The American military was trying to disguise our departure. There were roughly twelve hundred men going on this trip. So they put us up for maybe five or six days at Virginia

Beach, living like kings there. They didn't tell us anything. Most of us didn't know where we were going. But to disguise our departure further, they got some old trains that had been in mothballs. Old cars that were falling apart, and they sent a couple of these trains down, put us on board and we went off. We didn't know where we were going. We just rode all day on this train. I don't know where we were, it must have been three or four different states. And later that night they came back to Newport News, about midnight. And we'd been on this train zigzagging all over the countryside all day. This was to confuse the enemy. Maybe it did. It confused us.

"When we got there we saw the ship that was going was ready to take us on board—the *Château Thierry* it was called. It was an old ship that had been built in World War I, an old cargo vessel that had been refitted. A lot of us had little trunks, footlockers, but we couldn't take those aboard. We had to leave them on the dock, to be picked up by another boat on the convoy. They gave us a little pillow slip. The ship's officers told the men: 'Anything you can fit in there you can take on board, nothing else.' I had my recorder, my disc recorder. My friend Gordon MacCreagh had his bagpipes. And he had to leave them behind. That was a terrible blow to him. So we got aboard. They had bunks for us four and five tiers high and portholes on the sides. New, made-to-order sleeping accommodations. We were on our way to our first port—to Freetown, Sierra Leone. We had a convoy to take us across that Atlantic—including a very formidable collection of warships. The battleship *Texas* and a number of destroyers, probably four or five in our convoy. Going across there were probably eight vessels carrying cargo, personnel, something or other. We got to Freetown, and we had to spend a couple of days without being able to disembark. When we woke up in the morning to continue the voyage—all of our escort was gone, includ-

ing our battleship *Texas*! Actually the destroyers had sunk a couple of submarines on the way across. The subs had tried to get to us, but we felt very secure. With the battleship *Texas* how could you go wrong?"

▲▲

ON THE VOYAGE, Gordon MacCreagh became one of Courlander's good friends. "He had a background that was very interesting before I met him. He'd run guns into Ethiopia at the times that the Italians were invading, for which he had been decorated by the Ethiopian government. And that was how he got to know people in the government. His earlier life had been basically adventure. He was a professional adventurer. He used to go down to South America in search of something dangerous to do. He was looking for some very rare plants in Central America. It caused an international incident there because his visa was only good for one country. He came to a river that was the border of a different country, and he had no visa for that country. He solved that by digging up the stone border marking, putting it in his boat and taking it down the river, then setting it up again every night. They finally caught up with him and arrested him for sabotaging the border. He spent time in jail there, and had adventures in the mountains of Tibet. Gordon was a character. On the ship going over when we were talking about things, talking about the war, the Japanese, the Germans and so forth, he was a dissenter. He said, 'It's all big corporations, it's all economic stuff. It had nothing to do with all this stuff, fighting for democracy. It's just money fighting money, that's all.' "

The days on the ship dragged on. "We were approaching our destination, which we now knew would be Eritrea in Ethiopia. The

Soldiers, crowded in bunkers in the hold of the *Château Thierry,* cross the Atlantic in 1942 to serve in North Africa. *(Courtesy Courlander Family)*

convoy ahead of us going in the same direction had carried all the luggage we had left on the dock, among other things. They were going to the same port. But we learned as we approached the Straits of Madagascar that the Japanese subs were waiting for us up in the Straits. So we went out around and added about four or five days to the trip. We finally got to the port where we were going, Masawa, and somebody we knew was standing on the dock. I don't know how he got there ahead of us, but he said that the convoy ahead of us had been sunk in the Madagascar straits, and Gordon yelled '*My bagpipes!*' Of course that convoy had carried all our machine tools and everything but that was of no concern to him. 'My bagpipes!' Well it took me a little while to register, but I realized if his bagpipes went down then my recording equipment went down, too. When Gordon heard this news, his entire opinion of the war changed. His bagpipes went down and he became the most violent anti-Japanese man I ever saw in my life. . . .

"Eventually MacCreagh was able to get another set of bagpipes. Someone flying up to Cairo found some and brought them back. And then he started playing his bagpipes in the barracks, but he was evicted. Fourteen men in each barrack and they refused to listen to bagpipes—they sent him out. 'No bagpipes in the barracks!' So he was expelled with his bagpipes. He went out and sat on the rocks. We could hear his bagpipes in the distance. But it must have stirred something in the hearts of the hyenas because whenever he played the bagpipes all the hyenas began to yell."

Despite the sinking of their equipment convoy, Courlander and the men he traveled with arrived at their destination—the Gura airfield in Eritrea, which was then part of Ethiopia. In 1941, the British drove out the Italians and returned Haile Selassie, the exiled Ethiopian emperor, to the throne. The British were now stationed in

Ethiopia, but General Rommel, Hitler's commander of the North African forces of the Third Reich, was still a major threat. Courlander had picked up an Italian language book before leaving port, and on the the way over, managed to learn a number of words in Italian, mostly nouns. He thought it might prove useful. As it turned out, it was very useful indeed. Soon he became the "official interpreter" for the Americans with the Eritrean villagers, due to his knowedge of Italian nouns and his use of his own individual sign language.

Courlander and his comrades were placed to work on an operation mysteriously titled "Project 19." Working with the Douglas Aircraft Company, they were to find any planes that had been shot down in the area and take them back to the base, where men would take them apart and build new ones from the parts, so that they could be used again. There was also a hospital on base to care for wounded soldiers. At this time, Courlander became friends with Robert Kane, a talented artist who painted camouflage on Allied aircraft. Later, Kane would illustrate two of Courlander's folktale collections.

Courlander's first assignment was to work at the hospital, but soon the officers in charge learned that he was a writer. Part of the contract was to have someone document the project. Courlander became the official historian of "Project 19." One of the aspects of the historian's job was to learn something about "the general environment" of the area. The land around the base was dry and arid. Before the building of the airstrip, it had been home to several villages. Now the villagers had moved up into the surrounding mountains. Courlander decided that he would make it part of his job to get to know the people of the Eritrean countryside.

Although Eritrea is now a separate nation, when Courlander arrived there it was the northernmost province of Ethiopia, lying on the east coast of Africa between the Sudan and the Red Sea.

Ethiopia is a land of many peoples and many different languages. Its official language is Amharic, but in Eritrea, many of the people speak a language called Tigriña. Most of the elders of the villages spoke only their own language, but some of the younger people, especially children, had picked up Italian during the years of occupation. Courlander began to visit the Ethiopian villages. Often he would find himself speaking to the village elders through the oral interpreters, the children. A child would listen to Courlander's questions in Italian, and translate them into Tigriña to the elders. The leaders would answer and the child would respond to Courlander in Italian. Little by little Courlander began to study Tigriña as well. He never became as fluent in it as he did in Creole, but he did learn enough for basic communication. He kept a notebook with words and phrases in Tigriña to help himself learn the language.

Exploring a new land during wartime was a different experience for Courlander.

> We got off the ship and went off into the mountains, a couple of hours' drive, and got to our base in Gura. We arrived at the base on a Saturday night. On Sunday, the base managers gave the new troops a day off to explore and settle ourselves into the barracks. I decided I wanted to go off on my own, and to see what this new country was like. So in the mess hall I got a little extra breakfast food, put scrambled eggs between two slices of bread and put it in my pocket and didn't plan to be back anytime soon. I just went off in my own direction. It's fabulous country. It's on a plateau to start with, this area, but there were peaks all over and dry riverbeds, and very arid. It's sensational, to me it was. So I just kept walking and walking and didn't see a person all day.
>
> On the base we had Eritrean houseboys who would make up the beds in the barracks, and in the morning before I left I talked to one a little while and picked up a few phrases like greetings to people:

"*De hando aleka*" means, roughly translated, "How are you?" But he also gave me some rules, if it was an elderly person, a person of importance, you would phrase it a little differently: "*De hando alekum!*" and that's all through the language, that sort of thing. So I got a few of these phrases, as much as I could in fifteen or twenty minutes, before I left.

Somewhere around noon, it's a wild guess, I ate my egg sandwich. It must have been roughly two o'clock or something like that (I gauged the time from the sun), when I thought maybe I ought to start getting back. You know I'd spent all this time walking this way, that way, along the dry riverbed and the trail up the mountain. I decided it was time to come back, and I had just a kind of general idea from the sun where the base was. I must have been at that point about twenty miles out of the way. So I found a trail which seemed to go in that direction. I was following it. I went out beyond a big rock outcropping and then I found a party of elders having tea at the side of the trail there.

Again here was a little boy with them. We sort of greeted each other with signs and my bastard Italian, and the boy was helping the old folks with the Italian. And so we sat and they served me tea. I had a little cup. To strain the tea they poured it though a little ball of horsehair. It was my first tea in Ethiopia. And we talked again, they wanted to talk about America and when the war was over would the Italians come back, would the British take over? I couldn't tell them much that was helpful, but we were all getting along fine. Whenever I'd say something they'd nod as if they understood perfectly and then turn to the boy.

I got so that when they were talking to me in Tigriña I was nodding and turning to the boy, and everything filtered through him. Time came when I thought, Gee, I'd better get going. If I don't get back before dark I'll never get there, because I didn't know where I was. So I asked them, I told them where I had to go and could they

tell which would be the best way to go to get there. They indicated the general direction. The oldest man, he was probably about seventy-five, with a beard, was the elder of the group. So he took me by the hand and he led me a certain distance over to the beginning of a trail which went down steeply down the mountainside. And he indicated to keep going and follow that direction: "Go down this trail as far as the trail goes and then keep going."

I started down, and he was so genteel and friendly. He put up his hand and sort of blessed me on my way. And I thought, Gee, if I could only say something in his language. It would be kind of a gesture. I recalled one of these phrases I'd learned in the morning, which was not exactly appropriate. It was more a greeting than saying farewell, but I said it to him. He was blessing me on my way and then he heard this and he became transfixed. He recognized what I said, and I could see him looking this way and that—he was trying to think of something to reciprocate with in my language. So I stood there waving. Finally a big smile came on his face. He stood there, waved his hand in a kind of blessing, and uttered a two-word profanity in English. Here he was, a kindly old man. I don't know where he got that phrase from, probably the British soldiers or something. I was going down the hill and I think I had about twenty miles to go, but I was still laughing when I got back to the base.

▲▲

AS COURLANDER BEGAN to make excursions into the villages, he learned more about the Ethiopian people. Many of the villagers in Eritrea were Coptic Christians, whose rituals and beliefs dated back to biblical times. He also came into contact with the Falasha, or Beta Israel, who practice a form of Judaism that also dates back to ancient times. They strictly observe the laws and command-

Young girls in a village during one of Courlander's expeditions into the Ethiopian countryside in 1942. *(Courtesy the Center for Folklife Programs and Cultural Studies, Smithsonian Institution)*

ments written down in the Five Books of Moses. In the villages, Courlander saw much that impressed him. In these peoples' way of life, hospitality was not simply a word to be spoken, it was practiced. Travelers who had come from afar, whether friends or strangers, were always greeted warmly. Many times in his travels, he was welcomed into a villager's home. He was always given food, and it was a custom among the Ethiopian villagers to wash the feet of anyone who had traveled to see them. Later, in his novella *The Son of the Leopard*, he captured the feeling of these village traditions, the language and phrases, in an epic narrative. At the time, it was the immediacy of Courlander's experiences that drew him into the villagers' world.

In his diary he wrote: "Tigrai [Ethiopia and Eritrea] is a land that somehow remained itself though poisoned with a thousand inva-

sions. Each night, still the young children herd goats and other cattle upward from the tiny valleys to the forbidding hills upon which the villages cling, to keep them safe from bands of nocturnal brigands. Each night for more than two thousand years they have done this. Each year they have cultivated their fields and planted their grain, and every seventh year the elders have met in solemn council and redistributed the village lands."

The traditions Courlander saw were rich and complex, and reached back far into the distant past of North Africa and the Middle East. Even without a recorder, he began to document whatever he could of village life—church services and religious festivals, weddings, musical instruments, adult and children's games, children's

A priest shows Courlander and a young boy how to play the *nugarit*—a kettle-shaped drum—in Eritrea, 1942. *(Courtesy Courlander Family)*

songs and folktales. "The musical ways of these people are their own. . . . Even the dance steps and the singing style of Tigrai are of an old kind. When once you have heard an Abyssinian ballad or love-song sung to the accompaniment of the six-stringed lyre, or *masonquo,* you will never mistake it for the music of another place. Such songs David may well have sung in the temple, and Ethiopians swear that the harp David played was no other than the *masonquo* itself. Although there are drums, the rhythms are not African, but of the East. They are played in the churches by white-robed priests sitting cross-legged upon the floor. And priests summon their villagers to worship by sounding the ancient stone gongs or *döwel* that hang upon the sturdiest limbs of the weatherbeaten fig tree before the church doors."

Finally, at the base, a tape recorder was discovered in a bunker that the Italians had used as a cache for all kinds of equipment. Courlander did manage to record many of the songs and epics from the Eritrean villagers. He packed the tapes up carefully in two crates to be held in storage, but in the end, only one crate made it home after the war. (Still, he was later able to produce the songs in his recording *Folk Music of Ethiopia.*)

Once, in a village, he saw two elders huddled over a small wooden board. They were moving pieces around on it, and other villagers gathered around to watch. Courlander came close, too. He asked what they were doing, and a child said, "They are playing *gebeta.*"

"*Gebeta?*" asked Courlander. "What is that? How do you play?" He looked carefully at the board, but he couldn't figure out the rules.

Eventually, he was taught the game by a Sudanese man he had come to know, a craftsman who made drums and lyres—and *gebeta* boards. Courlander bought a set from him and learned to play. So he

was able to while away many hours in the village, sitting and playing *gebeta*, but all the time watching and listening to the goings-on around him. Maybe it was at such a time that he heard stories like this one, which later appeared in *The Fire on the Mountain and Other Ethiopian Stories:*

THE GAME BOARD

Once a man in the town of Nebri carved a beautiful gebeta *board for his son. He made it from the wood of an olive tree. When he was finished he showed his son how to play games upon it. The boy was very glad to have such a beautiful thing, and in the morning when he went out with the cattle to the valley where they grazed he took his* gebeta *board along. Everywhere he went, he carried his* gebeta *board under his arm.*

While he followed the cattle, he came upon a group of wandering Somalis with their camels, gathered around a small fire in a dry riverbed.

"Where in this country of yours can a man get wood?" the Somalis asked.

"Why, here is wood," the boy said. And he gave them the fine gebeta *board, which they put into the fire.*

As it went up in flames, the boy began to cry: "Oh, now where is my fine gebeta *board that my father has carved for me?"*

"Do not make such turmoil," the Somalis said, and they gave him a fine new knife in place of the game board.

The boy took the knife and went away with his cattle. As he wandered he came to a place where a man was digging a well in the sand of the riverbed, so that his goats could drink.

"The ground is hard," the man said. "Lend me your knife to dig with."

The boy gave the man the knife, but the man dug so vigorously with it that it broke.

"Ah, what has become of my knife?" the boy wailed.

An illustration by artist Robert Kane for "The Game Board," in *The Fire on the Mountain and Other Ethiopian Stories,* published in 1950. The man in the picture is carving a *gebeta* board. *(Courtesy Courlander Estate)*

"Quiet yourself," the man said: "Take this spear in its place." And he gave the boy a beautiful spear trimmed with silver and copper.

The boy went away with his cattle and his spear. He met a party of hunters. When they saw him one of them said:

"Lend me your spear, so that we may kill the lion we are trailing."

The boy gave him the spear, and the hunters went out and killed the lion. But in the hunt the shaft of the spear was splintered.

"See what you've done with my spear!" the boy cried.

"Don't carry on so," the hunter said. "Here is a horse for you in place of the spear."

The hunter gave him a horse with fine leather trappings, and he started back toward the village. On the way he came to where a group of workmen were repairing the highway. As they worked they caused a landslide, and the earth and rocks came down the mountain with a great roar. The horse became frightened and ran away.

"Where is my horse?" the boy cried. "You have made him run away!"

"Don't grieve," the workman said. "Here is an ax."

And he gave the boy a common iron ax.

The boy took the ax and continued toward the village. He came to a woodcutter who said:

"Lend me your ax for this tree. My ax is too small."

He loaned the woodcutter the ax, and the woodcutter chopped with it and broke it.

The boy cried, and the woodcutter said:

"Never mind, here is the limb of a tree."

The boy took the limb upon his back and when he came near the village a woman said:

"Where did you find the wood? I need it for my fire."

The boy gave it to her, and she put it in the fire. As it went up in flames he said:

"Now where is my wood?"

"Here," the woman said, "here is a fine gebeta *board."*

He took the gebeta *board under his arm and went home with the cattle. As he entered his house his father smiled and said:*

"What is better than a gebeta *game board to keep a small boy out of trouble?"*

▲▲

ONE DAY IN 1943, a small plane landed at the airstrip for refueling. Its passenger was Ephirem Towolde Medhen, the foreign minister of Emperor Haile Selassie's government in Addis Ababa. Medhen knew Gordon MacCreagh, or knew of him, because of his exploits in gunrunning for the Ethiopians, which had won him a citation from the emperor himself. MacCreagh told Medhen of some plans he had been thinking of for Ethiopia's economic development, specifically, an idea for building a dam on the Blue Nile near Lake Tana. He thought that

Courlander might have some useful ideas, too, but mostly MacCreagh was excited about the possibility of leaving the base and having another adventure. He asked Medhen to carry his ideas to the emperor. For a few weeks there was no reply, but one morning, the depot officer called them in with a message from Minister Medhen: "His Majesty Haile Selassie, Emperor of Ethiopia, requests your presence in two days to discuss matters of great importance to the Ethiopian government."

Courlander and MacCreagh had to report to the airfield the next day at four o'clock in the morning. Gordon was all set to go, but Courlander had a problem. He had his regular army outfits but no clothes suitable to wear to visit the emperor of Ethiopia. In desperation, he asked around the barracks and finally borrowed a gabardine suit from a friend. It wasn't until he got dressed to leave, stumbling around in the dark, that he realized he had a problem. The man he had borrowed the suit from was six feet tall and weighed 180 pounds, a good three sizes larger than himself! The pants were constantly slipping off his waist, and the arms of the jacket hung well below his hands. Still, at this point, he had no choice. Tugging his trousers up with the jacket slung over his arm, he made his way to the airstrip and boarded the plane.

After flying for hours over the deserts and the high mountain passes, with dizzying turns and dips, they landed in the airport of Addis Ababa, where Minister Medhen greeted them. After giving them a few minutes to wash and recover from their flight, Medhen took them to see the emperor. On the way, Gordon instructed Courlander on how one traditionally walked before the emperor. He explained to Courlander that one had to walk very carefully, taking one step forward, then bowing the head before taking another step forward.

"But of course," said Gordon, "we're Americans, and no one expects us to do this sort of thing. Just walk in a respectful and mannerly fashion." Courlander agreed.

When Medhen brought them before Haile Selassie, the ruler had just recently awakened from his afternoon nap. He sat at his desk. At his feet were two huge Great Danes, lying on the rug. By chance Courlander entered first, and so walked in with what he considered to be his most respectful stride up to the emperor. When he turned around, he saw that Gordon had chosen to walk one step at a time, with his head bowing at each step. Just to look better and more schooled than me! thought Courlander. Well, I'll talk to him about that later!

Selassie was a small man. Courlander had seen him often on newsreels when he had pleaded for the League of Nations to take action against the invasion of his country. Years later, Courlander wrote:

Haile Selassie, emperor of Ethiopia, in full military dress, c. 1940. *(Courtesy the New York Public Library, Office of Special Collections)*

"His face was that of a genial grandfather. . . . Something about him made him seem larger than life, and this impression never left me."

Selassie spent an hour with the two men. He told them about the many challenges facing his country: the lack of resources, made worse by the British, who directed every item they needed toward the war effort. He told Courlander that the Italians had killed many of the brightest and best of the young Ethiopian intellectuals who had studied in Western universities. Now the country needed teachers, people who could speak the different languages of the indigenous peoples—Amharic, Galla, Somali—and would be able to help Ethiopians achieve full literacy. Courlander, who knew people through his research and his work with foundations, said that he would try to help.

Gordon then spoke to the emperor of his dream project, which he thought would do the most to help the country: building a dam at Lake Tana. Gordon had all sorts of ideas that he presented to Selassie about how he would lobby for the project and find the funds, architects, and builders. Selassie smiled. He knew Gordon a little. "And if we build this dam, my friend, what share would you like to have in it?"

"Your Majesty," Gordon replied, "when the dam is under construction, I would like to have the hot dog concession."

"Very well, Mr. MacCreagh—we'll talk about it when the time comes."

Their visit at an end, Courlander turned around and walked toward the door. Gordon was behind him. As Courlander stood at the door, he saw that Gordon, still showing off his courtly manners, was walking backward, one step at a time, with his head bowed, heading straight toward one of the Great Danes lying on the carpet. "I could have warned him, but I felt that a cosmic act of justice was about to take place, in the presence of which I was nothing but a

mere mortal witness. It was like a slow-motion dream. Two more backward steps and two more inclinations of his head, and Gordon fell over the dog. He was lying on his back with his feet in the air. Both dogs leaped at him, and one had his teeth in Gordon's sleeve. The Emperor jumped up, ran around the desk, and pulled the dogs off. I don't remember what was said, only the sound of Gordon giggling, and the sight of him now going *forward* toward the door—an unconventional ending to a royal audience. I no longer felt the need to speak to Gordon about the one step forward-backward business."

There were several more visits planned with Selassie as well as other high-level officials in Addis Ababa, but the plane from Gura could not stay any longer. Medhen assured the two that he would find transportation for them back to Eritrea, and so they argreed to stay in the capital city. One afternoon, they roamed the marketplace, where Courlander found some cut-glass beads and a leopard skin to bring back to the base. As it turned out, there were no other planes available for two American soldiers who had no official business with the British, so they had to return in a somewhat dilapidated jeep. The driver was a paymaster on Medhen's staff. A fifteen-year-old boy, the son of a Baptist missionary in Amhara, rode with them and four soldiers rode in a jeep behind them, for protection.

On the way back, on one of the big mountain passes, they saw ahead a crowd of about 150 men carrying rifles and waving. These could have been *shiftas,* bandits and outlaws who roamed the back-country of Ethiopia, or possibly their jeeps had been mistaken for an enemy convoy! In either case, there was no way out. A tall cliff was on one side of the road and a sheer drop-off on the other. Courlander turned around to signal the soldiers behind them, but all four of them had disappeared, leaving their jeep empty. It was too late to turn back, and the driver had only his .22-caliber rifle as a weapon. The

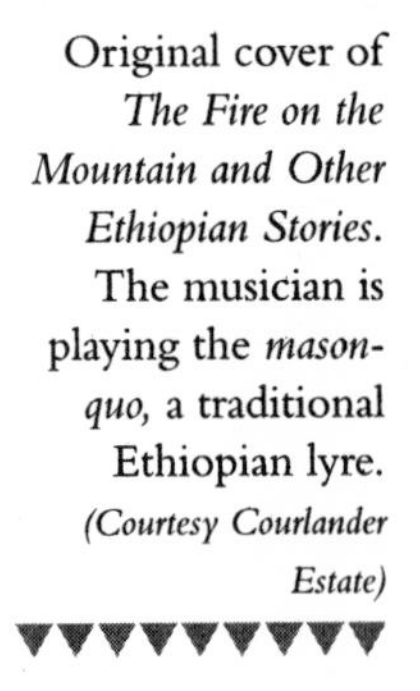

Original cover of *The Fire on the Mountain and Other Ethiopian Stories*. The musician is playing the *mason-quo,* a traditional Ethiopian lyre. *(Courtesy Courlander Estate)*

men swarmed toward them; some were carrying guns, while others were carrying traditional shields and swords. To Courlander's amazement, they simply ran around them, and then made their way down the steep precipice, without a backward glance to the jeep. Soon after, the four soldiers "guarding them" returned to their vehicle. In the distance, they saw a small village, and when they reached it, the villagers told them that the men they had seen were a raiding party, carrying out a vendetta against another village some miles away.

In Adigrat, a small city, MacCreagh and Courlander found their way to the public bus, and in several hours they were dropped off near the Gura airfield. A few days later, the entire company received orders. The tour in Ethiopia had come to an end. The next plane Courlander boarded was to carry him back to the United States. But the war was still in progress, and the future uncertain.

CHAPTER 6

BOMBAY

COURLANDER'S RETURN TO THE UNITED STATES WAS BRIEF. He did have time, however, to see Ella and their daughter, Erika—his firstborn child, now a year old. But in short order, he appeared before the draft board again. This time, members of the Office of War Information (OWI) requested his services as a journalist and foreign correspondent. Although he was ready to join for combat at any time, the OWI needed his expertise, and so it was that once again he flew out of the country. This time he was sent to India, to the city of Bombay. At the time, the British still controlled the vast subcontinent. But the struggle for independence from the great colonial empires was gathering steam—not only in India, but in many other countries around the world. As the Allies fought against the tyranny of the Axis powers, many nations looked forward to the day when they could earn their own freedom from the Allies.

In a passage from a letter to Melville Herskovits that he sent from Michigan in 1941, Courlander wrote his thoughts about the war, and

colonialism: "No one would rather see a finish to the British Empire than I, but certainly not when it means the victory of Hitlerism and all that implies. One step at a time. Hitlerism first. Then Empirism. One trembles to think how long the conflict may last."

And so this idealistic young American found himself seeing firsthand life under colonial rule. In Bombay, Courlander could do little recording and research. Most of his time was taken up with his assignments for the OWI. But this in itself afforded him opportunities to see and meet people from many walks of life. In India, Courlander came face-to-face with hierarchies of power and privilege that operated on many levels, ones that were different from those he had seen in his own country and the Caribbean.

The British had imposed their own rules and regulations on Indian society, which applied to native Indians and foreigners alike. Once, Courlander and a coworker, Jim Daniel, thought they might stop at a nice hotel, called the Hotel Taj Mahal, for a special meal. They were let in, but for the British, dress codes and appearances were an important matter. The two Americans were served a meal, but they were hidden behind a screen so that people of "quality"—the well-dressed upper-class British—wouldn't have to look at them. The Indian population was subject to many such indignities and worse. But Courlander observed, too, that the Indians had their own rigid structure, the caste system, which dates back centuries, long before the arrival of the British. Although he had seen racism and economic injustice aplenty in the United States and the Caribbean, the system of categorizing people in India was something new to him, and it offended his own sense of values on a very deep level.

One day, he and Jim were working in their office. They needed to see some financial papers and called upstairs to one of their office staff, a native-born Indian. Would he bring down the papers? A few minutes went by, then fifteen minutes, then half an hour, but

Courlander (near the window) and fellow workers at the Bombay office of the Office of War Information (OWI), 1944. *(Courtesy Courlander Family)*

the man didn't appear. Finally they called up to him again, and he replied: "I'm not coming down yet. I haven't found anyone to carry my ledger book." Being a Brahmin, a descendant of the priestly high class, he was not allowed to perform a task of this nature, although the ledger book itself was quite small. There were some other people who worked in the office area, but they were of the untouchables, the lowest class. The Brahmin could not give the ledger to one of them, because any contact between them was forbidden. Finally Courlander ran up to get the ledger, but he never forgot his sense of amazement. To Harold Courlander, educated to the American ideals, if not realities, of social democracy, these attitudes were hard to understand, much less sympathize with.

An ancient Indian folktale, which Courlander later collected and retold in *The Tiger's Whisker and Other Tales from Asia and the Pacific*, makes its own point about class prejudice.

BOMBAY

THE SCHOLARS AND THE LION

(An Indian Tale)

There were once four men who were friends. Three of them were wise and learned in books. But the fourth was not a scholar. All he had was common sense.

It happened once that the four men were conversing together. They spoke of how nice it would be to travel to far-off places and see something of the world. "What good are books if we can't go places and apply our learning to the things around us?" one of them said. "Yes," the others said, "the learning we have acquired is much too great to be applied to this little village."

So they prepared themselves with clothes and food and began their journey. And after a while, when they were trudging along the road, one of the three learned men declared:

"I have been thinking. Three of us have spent our lives in study. We have pored through books. We have sat up late at night, reading by the light of our oil lamps until our eyes have closed with weariness. Now we are going out into the world to make our knowledge useful. With the things we have learned we will become rich. Yet there is a fourth man with us, our unlearned friend. Has he studied and prepared for this day? No, he contributes nothing at all to our expedition. Why should he come along and share our hard-earned good luck?"

The second scholar thought and answered: "These are wise and just words." He turned to the unlearned man and said to him: "Good friend, you are no scholar. Please leave us and go home."

The third scholar spoke. He said: "No, this isn't right. He is no scholar, as we all know. But he has been our friend since childhood. Let him come and share with us the great treasures we are going to discover through our wisdom."

They finally decided that their unlearned friend could come along and share with them, even though he had nothing at all to contribute but common sense.

The four men resumed their journey, traveling from place to place in search of wealth and fortune. They passed through a forest, and came to a clearing

Artist Enrico Arno's illustration of "The Scholars and the Lion," in *The Tiger's Whisker and Other Tales from Asia and the Pacific,* first published in 1959. *(Courtesy Courlander Estate)*

where the bones of a dead lion were scattered on the ground. They stood looking at the bones of the dead animal. One of the scholars said:

"See what a wonderful opportunity lies here before us. With these bones we can test the value of our learning. Isn't our great scholarship able to bring this creature back to life? For my part, I can assemble the bones of the animal, each in its right place."

The second scholar said: "I too have learning on this subject. I can cover the bones with flesh, blood, and skin."

And the third scholar said: "As for me, I can give this creature life and make it breathe."

The fourth man, who was no scholar at all, was humble and silent before such tremendous learning.

So the first scholar assembled the bones of the lion and put them together. The second scholar put a covering of flesh and skin over the lion, and put blood in the body. Then the third scholar began the business of bringing the lion to life.

At this moment the fourth man, the fellow without any learning in his head, protested vigorously. He said:

"My dear friends, think what you are about to do! This animal that you are bringing back to life is a lion! If you are successful, he will rise up and kill us all!"

The third scholar, busily applying all his hard-won knowledge, shouted: "What good is learning if it isn't applied to things?"

"I plead with you, think again!" the fourth man said. "But if you are really determined to go through with it, at least wait until I have climbed a tree!"

He scurried up a tall tree and sat in the branches. Then the third scholar resumed his work of bringing the dead lion to life, while the two other scholars stood close by, observing everything he did with the greatest of interest. The third scholar stepped back in triumph.

"It is done!" he exclaimed proudly.

The lion opened its eyes, switched its tail nervously, and got to its feet. And then without warning, it sprang upon the three learned men and killed them.

The fourth man, the one who had never studied books, waited in the tree until the lion had gone away. Then he came down and returned alone to his village.

And so it is that people say:

> *"Scholarship's no substitute for common sense*
> *Attain, if you can, intelligence.*
> *Three senseless scholars lost in pride*
> *Made a lion—then they died."*

Courlander himself was quite comfortable with the many people he met who were in the "untouchable" caste. To him, they were more human, more real, and easier to communicate with than highly placed Brahmins.

At this time, Mohandas Gandhi was bringing a similar message of tolerance to all Indians, even as he was building a great nonviolent campaign for independence. Ten years later an American, Dr. Martin Luther King, Jr., began to apply Gandhi's ideas to challenge racism and segregation in the United States.

As in Haiti, Courlander's interests and sympathies became known by word of mouth in Bombay. One day, a young man, who worked as a *hamal,* a housekeeper, came to Courlander with an invitation. "My uncle wants you to come to a meeting," he said, "a special meeting. My uncle has heard of you and he wishes you to come."

Courlander agreed to go. He and an American companion followed the young man into the city. Finally they arrived at a house. It was evening by now. Inside a large room with low ceilings sat rows of men and women. They were all untouchables. Many were singing songs, beating out rhythms with small drums and rattles. The young man's uncle greeted his guests, and then he began to speak. He

spoke of their need for liberation and freedom. The singing and drumming went on for many hours. Although Courlander could not understand every word that was spoken, he understood the underlying message.

A few weeks later, Jim Daniel decided that the OWI should have a picnic for all the people who worked with them. Indians and British, lower and upper caste. He thought it might help "break the ice." The picnic day was planned: they would all go boating to Elephanta Island, an enchanting island outside the city known for its caves covered with ancient frescoes and bas-relief sculpture. When everyone had gathered at the docks, the boats pulled up for the passengers to board. The OWI had provided baskets of food and drink for everyone. The baskets lay on the pier. Nobody went to pick them up. Then one, two, three young men went to the baskets and put them on their heads.

Slowly they walked toward the boats. These young men were untouchables, the only ones deemed fit to carry the baskets. Courlander and Jim Daniel looked at each other. They knew very well what was going on, and what they were each thinking. Without saying a word they, too, went over to the docks and picked up baskets and, putting them on their heads, began to carry them to the waiting boats. The Indian guests were in consternation. This kind of work was for untouchables only! It was bad enough they were coming to the picnic at all! What were these Americans thinking of?

Daniel and Courlander explained, "In America, everybody shares. If there is carrying to be done, everybody could do it, anybody could do it." One by one, each of the guests picked up a basket and moved onto the boats. The picnic went on as planned, and everyone had a good time. Whether or not this incident changed the lives of anyone of either the untouchables or the Brahmins who had been there is hard to say, but it was an incident that for Courlander evoked the time and social realities of the people he was meeting and working with during his months in Bombay.

Courlander's stay in India was not long—a six-month tenure out of his three years with the OWI. He did not record or do any formal research there in folk traditions. Nevertheless, the experience provided him with a deeper sense of the workings of history, class, and political power in another part of the world as the British empire was coming to a close and an independent nation was beginning to emerge. He saw, too, how groups of people, like the untouchables, used the power of music, dance, and song to give them hope and strength as they fought for a better future.

His work with the OWI also afforded him some opportunity to see other parts of Asia. Courlander traveled to Egypt, Jordan, and Palestine. He also had a chance to visit, at last, Nigeria and Ghana, along the west coast of Africa, as well as the Sudan. In 1945, the war ended. Courlander returned to New York City. Victory for the Allies had come, and people in the United States had to adjust now to the realities of a post–World War II era that was just beginning to unfold—the realignment of power in Eastern and Western Europe; the realization by the world of the unspeakable events of the Holocaust; and the advent of the atomic bomb and the potential in the future for nations to engage in nuclear warfare.

The end of the war also signaled a change in Courlander's personal life. He and Ella divorced. She took custody of their daughter and moved back to the Midwest. Courlander stayed in New York and took on a new job as feature editor with the Voice of America, a government agency devoted to communicating by radio what life was like in the United States to countries in Europe, Asia, and Africa. World War II had ended, but the Cold War was just beginning, and many changes were ahead for Courlander and the country.

CHAPTER 7

FOLKWAYS AND THE SOUTH

MOSES ASCH, OR MOE ASCH as he came to be known, was a man with a dream. His dream was to record all the sounds of the world's peoples—their music, their poetry, their songs—as a legacy for future generations. Starting off in a tiny office in New York's East Village, he found enough money to start a recording studio and began to record and distribute his titles. Little by little, he gathered around him a group of singers and artists whose names are now legend in American music: Woody Guthrie, Pete Seeger, Leadbelly, Odetta, and poets like Langston Hughes and Gwendolyn Brooks. Moe needed people to work with him who not only were good at music recording but also understood different cultures. He needed people who were willing to put their time into tracking down and listening to field recordings from the rain forest of Brazil to the deserts of Morocco.

In 1947, Harold Courlander, still working in in New York with the Voice of America, met with Moe Asch. Soon he came on board

Moses Asch and Harold Courlander at the Folkways office in New York City, early 1960s. *(Courtesy David Gahr)*

to work, helping Asch to build his fledgling collection of music from around the world. The company had had a few names but none stuck, until one day Courlander said, "Why don't you call it Folkways?"

Moe liked the name, and the next recording had the Folkways label. Courlander knew enough about recording to help Moe set up his studio so that it would work efficiently and well. He also had a number of his own field recordings that soon became part of the Folkways catalog. His early recordings in Haiti and Cuba became the records *Music of Haiti* (volumes 1 and 2) and *Cult Music of Cuba*. Each Folkways record had extensive notes to explain the words and meanings of the songs. Courlander wrote and edited not only for his own records, but for others as well. And he helped Moe in the area of authenticity. Was this a true field recording or just someone playing in his backyard? Soon, Courlander became the editor of Ethnic Folkways, the division of Folkways that was devoted to world music.

To find recordings, he corresponded with people all over the world. Here is a letter that he wrote to a friend who was stationed in Morocco, at the beginning of his work with Moe, in 1943:

FOLKWAYS RECORDS AND SERVICE CORP.
117 West 46th St.
New York, N.Y.

March 31, 1943

Dear Wynn:

It was good to hear from you and to know that you have not been swallowed up by the Atlas Mountains. In my mind they as foreboding a bunch of mountains as I know. Not that I was actually in them, but only over them. The worst airplane ride I ever had was at night, in a storm, in a battered C-46, over the Atlas Range. I'm sure they are a lot different in the sunshine, with both of one's feet on solid ground.

Your description of your living quarters on Djemaa-el-fna gives me the wanderlust! By all means record those various street sounds, close-up if possible. Street cries, drums, snake charmer, water seller and all—not forgetting the muezzins before dawn!

Recordings of the groups you refer to as "semi-professionals" will be very useful. I assume they do traditional things. All the stuff you mention is interesting. Don't forget the dances, ballads, love songs, worksongs, et al. Don't forget children's game songs, and some of those wandering musicians of various sorts that show up and perform in the streets.

Documentation is extremely important. You are working in an area where relatively little work of this sort has been done. Get as much information as you can on each performer and piece. As to

performer; name if possible; whether Negro, Berber, Arab, or whatnot, and from where or what tribe; and pictures if possible of the performers—candid, in action if you can catch them; close-up pics of instruments, or player and instrument together; names of instruments. As to the separate pieces, get whatever you can of the type of piece, what it means, when it is played or sung, and from time to time a translation will help.

I'm looking forward to hearing the first tapes! In reply to some of the specific questions:

Mr. Asch, Production Chief at Folkways, is sending you a batch of tapes, addressed to Cpl. John Snelling. He is sending the 7″ tapes, as they will be easier for you to handle. When you've used them up and need more, holler. Mr. Asch informs me there is a 12-volt generator available which could be used with your car battery in connection with field trips. I'll investigate price, etc., and let you know.

Let's hear from you when there's news. And we're eager to hear some of that music from Marrakech and environs!

Kindest regards,
Harold Courlander

When Moe died at the age of eighty-four, the Folkways collection was turned over to the Smithsonian Institution. In a 1985 letter to the Smithsonian, Courlander wrote: ". . . the cultural value of the published and unpublished items collectively known as Folkways is, in my opinion, enormous." Today there are over two thousand records in the collection with new publications and recordings being produced every year. Folkways did become the national legacy that Moe had always wanted it to be.

Courlander was enjoying his work with Folkways and the Voice of America, but his heart was in his field research and his own writing.

He had spent a lot of time in the Caribbean. He had been to Ethiopia and had had a chance to visit West Africa. Now, he felt, it was time to learn about the people who had started him off in this direction in the first place. The children he had played with in Detroit school yards, whose parents had come up North to look for better work and opportunities, brought with them the black culture of the South. Their songs and music had inspired his writing from his earliest days, when he wrote *Swamp Mud* and *Home to Langford County.* It was time to look for the voices at home, and see how they, too, might be connected to the cultures of Africa and of Africans all around the world.

In 1949, under the auspices of the Wenner-Gren Foundation, Harold Courlander made his first lengthy trip to the American South. With him was his second wife, the former Emma Meltzer. Emma was an aspiring artist he had met when he was working at the OWI. They were married on June 18, 1949. She accompanied him on many of his field trips during the 1950s and in later years as well.

Courlander had to decide where he would go to do his work. After some thought and study, he chose to go to the area of Sumter County in Alabama, near the town of Livingston. Later he would move on to Mississippi and Louisiana as well. He wanted to go to places where he knew the oral tradition would be alive and still a vital part of the black community. He had a sense that in this particular part of the South he would find what he was looking for and would learn what he was hoping to learn.

Alabama in the 1950s was a place where the reality of racism in America was in full view. Jim Crow laws forbade blacks and whites from eating in the same restaurants, drinking water from the same water fountains, sending their children to the same schools. The Courlanders' first stop was at Tuskegee Institute, the college in

Alabama founded in 1881 by the influential black leader and educator Booker T. Washington. There he met with several scholars who helped direct him in his research. Then they traveled on to Sumter County.

On one of his first days in Livingston, Courlander wanted to find a certain woman whom he had heard was an excellent singer. She was also a teacher. He went to the Livingston Board of Education to find out how to contact her. The secretary looked up the teacher's name in the file and said, "Oh, to find her, you'll have to go to the *other* Board of Education." In Selma, Alabama, a city he visited during his first days, he saw how much of the work of the city, such as manufacturing and construction, was being done by black men and women. Yet it was only white people who walked the main streets, who entered the shops and office buildings. He asked a black man he knew, "Why don't black people walk on the main street? Aren't they allowed?"

The man answered him, "Oh, they're allowed, but they know better." Courlander realized that some of the laws separating the races were written, plain to see, while others were unspoken, hidden, but just as strongly felt. For Courlander, it was only fitting that Alabama would become the fiery center of the civil rights movement in 1955, when Rosa Parks made her stand against Jim Crow and Martin Luther King, Jr., led the Montgomery bus boycott.

By the mid-1950s, stirrings of social change were already taking hold. The NAACP was bringing legal pressure in Alabama and Mississippi to end segregation in the school system, and to give blacks voting rights. Many white southerners were distrustful of Courlander, as they were of anyone from the North who was interested in mingling with people in the black community. But there were exceptions. One of the people who helped Courlander find his way in Alabama was an elderly white woman named Ruby Pickens Tartt. She was a folklorist in her own right, and her father, a high-

ranking member of the state government, had always been interested in black music. When she was a child, he took Ruby with him to black churches and camp meetings. During the Roosevelt years and the Depression, Ruby was asked to document songs and traditions of the black community as part of a government-sponsored oral history project, the Federal Writers' Project. Later, Ruby worked with the renowned folklorist John Lomax and his son, Alan Lomax, on their song-collecting projects. Many of the songs they recorded are now part of the Archive of Folk Song in the Library of Congress.

Ruby knew how to find some of the best blues and gospel singers in Sumter County. One of them was a man named Red Willie. Red Willie had come to Alabama from the Sea Islands off the coast of Georgia. He was known for his singing and guitar playing. He lived in back of a lumberyard on the outskirts of town. Ruby agreed to take Harold and Emma out to the lumberyard so they could meet Red Willie. They wanted to set up a time to talk to him, and, they hoped, to record.

When they arrived at the lumberyard, Red Willie wasn't there. His wife was home, however, so they decided to wait for him. As they sat in their car, they heard the sound of another vehicle pulling into the yard. They expected to see Red Willie, but instead they saw a truck. "It was a pickup truck with three men—they had one big bottle they had been sharing, Southern Comfort or whatever it was. It was obviously a father and two sons. So they just drove up and were all looking at me. There I was sitting on the steps of Red Willie's shack. I had out-of-state plates on my car. So I went up to them. I didn't wait for them. One of them said, 'Are you one of them damn Yankees coming down here to stir up trouble?'

"I said, 'Well, I don't know if you can call me a Yankee or not. I wasn't really born as a Yankee. I was born out in the Middle West. I've lived in a lot of places. I live in the state of New York now, and

Red Willie (Willie Turner), one of the musicians Courlander met and recorded during his fieldwork in Alabama in 1952. *(Photo: Harold Courlander. Courtesy the Center for Folklife Programs and Cultural Studies, Smithsonian Institution)*

I didn't come here to stir up any trouble.' They were very suspicious of me. and the father said, 'What are you doing out here at Red Willie's place?' I said, 'Waiting for Red Willie.'

"They felt very free to ask me all of these questions that were none of their business. I was very open. I said, 'I'm here collecting music from your area, and I was told that Red Willie was a good blues singer and I wanted to come out and see what songs he had.' The man stopped. He said, 'Red Willie sings the blues?' The tide had turned already. I said, 'Yeah, that's what I'm told,' and the next thing he was silent for a while and then he offered me the bottle. I don't know what it was but I drank it out of the bottle as if I did that every day. Ruby and my wife were sitting in our car. Ruby was terrified. She was nervous about a confrontation with these people." Ruby knew that these were the type of people who didn't want any strangers, especially strangers from the North, interfering with their way of life. Sometimes their resentment could turn to open hostility, or worse. But Courlander remained calm, and eventually, their manner became more friendly.

" 'I'll be damned,' said the one who was the driver. 'I didn't know that Red Willie could sing the blues.'

"After hearing this, the one who was driving said to his companions, 'Let's go into town. I know where we can find him.' They drove off in the car, weaving this way and that way. They never came back. By the time they got to town they forgot all about it I'm sure. Anyway, Red Willie showed up. We made a date. We talked a lot. And at the appointed time I took him somewhere else where we wouldn't be disturbed by people like these, and I recorded quite a few of his songs."

Here is one of the songs, "Baby Please Don't Go," that Courlander recorded from Red Willie:

Baby please don't go, (×3)
Back to Baltimore,
Baby please don't go.

Turn your lamp down low, (×3)
And baby please don't go,
Baby please don't go.

You know I loves you so, (×3)
And baby please don't go,
Baby please don't go.

I beg you all night long, (×3)
And night before,
Baby please don't go.

Now your man done come, (×3)
From the county farm,
Now your man done come.

Rich Amerson—storyteller, preacher, ballad singer—whom Courlander met and worked with during his research in Alabama. *(Courtesy Smithsonian/Folkways Archives)*

I'm goin' to walk your log, (×2)
And if you throw me off
I'm goin' to walk your log.

Courlander spent many hours looking for and finding people he could work with. And he met them: singers and storytellers, preachers, farmers, workers in towns, and traveling men. As he began to record and listen, he began to see that the songs of black people were not made up of isolated melodies and words. Rather, they were all connected to broad themes of life and beliefs. Spirituals were an entire oral literature of the Bible, the Old and New Testaments. In the black churches, each story in the Bible had been interpreted with a song. Each of these songs talked about the Bible story from

the feelings and perspectives of black people. Courlander also found this continuity expressed, with different themes, in the hard-edged blues ballads, work songs, and children's games that he documented in his book *Negro Folk Music U.S.A.*

Of all the people Courlander met in Alabama, the one who deeply inspired him was Rich Amerson. Rich Amerson, born and raised in Sumter County, was a true people's bard. He worked at his farm but he also traveled. He was a singer, storyteller, philosopher, and preacher—all in one. When Rich told a story, everyone paid attention, and he always had the right story for the occasion. In his memoir "Recording in Alabama in 1950," Courlander wrote about Amerson: "He was often somewhere on the road with his bicycle, searching for short-term jobs and new experiences. He worked variously as a track liner, caller (singer, rhythm-keeper, and exhorter for track crews), and digger of storm pits. He also dug wells and specialized as a "well taster" (to determine if the water was potable).

In small towns along his route of passage, Amerson sang on street corners, danced, played his mouth harp, told stories, and preached his own dramatic version of biblical texts. He seemed to know the Bible by heart. Sometimes a small church would call on him for a sermon. His voice was not smooth or cultivated, but it was tone-true, had marvelous subtleties and nuances, and was dramatically compelling. When he sang religious songs, he often introduced them with relevant biblical preachments. His storytelling was eloquent, whether he told of actual happenings, apocryphal events, personal adventures, or Buh Rabbit tales. Amerson had no schooling, but he was a natural-born entertainer. He sometimes said, "I was schooled in hard work and I read with a hoe and write with a plow." His voice can be heard on volumes three and four of the six-volume recording that Courlander released through Folkways called *Negro Folk Music of Alabama*.

Rich Amerson continued to resonate in Courlander's mind and imagination long after his research had ended. Somehow, just collecting his stories and his songs wasn't enough. Rich's life meant something more than that; his life in itself told a story. And so Courlander wrote the novel *The Big Old World of Richard Creeks,* which was published in 1962. The book is written in the voice of Richard Creeks, giving his view of life for black people in the South of the pre–civil rights era: "I can't read books that other folks [have] written, cause I'm poor in schooling, but I been around a long time and seen a lot of things, and you might say I am kind of a book myself. And the way it seems to me, there is some white folks is only happy trying to keep things the way they used to be. I don't know no Negroes that want it that way, though, and there's more and more of them don't want it the way it *is,* either. Some of them goes North to do better, but there's a mess of them says it's got to be better right

Rich Amerson with his sister, Earthy Anne Coleman (left), and Sarah Amerson in Livingston, Alabama. *(Photo: Harold Courlander. Courtesy Courlander Family)*

here." If you read the book carefully, you'll see that Courlander created fictional characters based on many of the people he had met in the South, including Ruby Pickens Tartt (he called her Miss Judy), and even himself, as an itinerant song collector from "up North."

In the book, Courlander drew on much of the research he did in the South. Lyrics of blues and work songs and folk beliefs that Amerson and others had shared with Courlander run through the story. Courlander was bringing together what he knew and understood of the social picture of the black South, through the voice of one man—Richard Creeks. Writing the novel also gave him a way to interpret and make sense of what he had seen and experienced. In one way, it was a book that sought to represent a culture or group of people: the rural communities of the black South. In another way, it was his own response to a complex social experience. Courlander was both speaking for people whose stories would otherwise go unheard outside of their communities and telling his own stories through theirs.

▲▲

TIME AND TIME AGAIN in the stories and songs of the black people of Alabama and Mississippi, Courlander found connections to the music he'd heard in Haiti, in Cuba, and in West Africa. Anansi the Spider is one of the trickster characters best known by the Akan-speaking people of Ghana. In one of those stories, still told today, Anansi the Spider wants to keep all the wisdom in the world to himself. He gathers the wisdom from all the creatures of the earth and puts it into a big iron pot. He ties the pot around his stomach and tries to take it up into a high tree, where no one else will find it. As he struggles up the tree, his son, Ntikuma, comes along and suggests

that his father put the pot on his back. Angered that his little son knows better than he how to take the pot up the tree, Anansi throws it down and wisdom once again spreads all over the world. That is why everyone has at least a little bit of wisdom. As the proverb of the story says, "one head can't exchange ideas with itself."

In Alabama one evening, as he sat and recorded Rich Amerson and his sister, Earthy Anne, Courlander heard this tale, which he included in his collection *Terrapin's Pot of Sense:*

Now just why you think it is all the critters got different kinds *of sense, and different amounts too? 'Tain't merely on account of they got a shape like a rabbit or turkey or a water snake. There's somethin' behind it all, and right now it's what I'm goin' to talk about.*

In the old days they was a big competition 'mongst the animals to see which one of 'em could collect the most good sense. Buh Coon, Buh Fox, Buh Guinea, Buh Geese, Buh Snake, and all the others went runnin' around pickin' up pieces of good sense on the ground or on the bushes or wherever they could find 'em. Buh Coon had a little pile of good sense in his place, Buh Rabbit had a little pile in his place, Buh Rooster had some in his place. Of course, they was all in such a hurry to outdo the other folks that some of the sense they picked up wasn't so good, and some was downright spoiled. But everyone was braggin' 'bout what a pile of sense he had back home. Trouble was, the places they had to keep it wasn't just right. Buh Possum's house had a leak in the roof, and everytime it rained, the water came drip, drip, drip, down on Possum's pile of sense. Buh 'Gator he put his sense in the nest where he keep his eggs, but every time the young ones hatch out they jump around and kick the good sense all over the place. Buh Rooster have his good sense in a nice pretty pile, but his wife, Sister Hen she's so nearsighted she can't tell sense from corn, and she was always a-peckin' at it. Buh Duck he want to fly South in the winter and don't know what to do with his pile of sense.

Well, Buh Terrapin he got a fine idea. He say, "Friends, what we need is a caretaker to take care of all the sense we gathered. You just bring it to me and I'll be the caretaker."

All the animals liked that idea, 'cause it eased their worries for 'em. So they all brought the sense they'd collected to Buh Terrapin, and he gave each and every one of 'em a receipt for it. Then he took all that sense and put it in a big iron cookin' pot.

Afterward he begin to study where could he hang the pot. At last he decided he goin' to hang it top of a great big sycamore tree safe and sound. So he took the pot in front of him and went to climb the tree with it. But he got a powerful problem, 'cause the pot was pretty big and Terrapin's legs was too short in the first place to be climbin' trees. Took Terrapin most of the day to get halfway up. All the critters was standin' around watchin' that pot of sense go up, sayin', "Hey there, Buh Terrapin, careful of that pot! It got my sense in it!"

Just afore nightfall a wind come up and begin blowin' things around. The top of the sycamore tree began to switch back and forth. Wind got stronger, and the top of the tree commence to whippin' around till Buh Terrapin couldn't hold on no more. He hollered, "Here I come!" and let go.

Buh Terrapin landed smack on his back and lay right there where he fall. The iron pot hit the ground and rolled this way and that. Naturally, everything that was in it got scattered all over. All the critters started to run around pickin' up pieces of sense. Everything was mixed up, and couldn't no one tell which was his and which was somebody else's. Didn't have time then to figure out what was good sense, or ordinary sense, or plain stupidity—everybody just grabbed.

And when they had they hands full and didn't know what to do with it, Buh Horse say, "I don't know what all you folks doin' with yours, but I'm puttin' mine in my head." And when he did that, the others say, "I'm puttin' mine in my head too," and they did the same as Buh Horse did.

That's how come all the critters got sense in their heads. And they got good sense and bad sense as well. Some's luckier than others in what they picked up. Mostly everybody got a mixture, though.

When that part of it was all over, they saw Buh Terrapin still on his back, and they righted him. They saw his shell was all cracked from fallin' on the ground, just the way it's been ever since. They went away and left him. Terrapin he crawled around in the grass lookin' for bits of sense they'd left behind. He found some, but they hadn't left much for him. When you see Buh Terrapin crawlin' around in the grass nowadays, you can figure he's still lookin' for some scraps of sense.

That's a sad story for Buh Terrapin, ain't it? But some folks figure he had it comin', on account of they think he was fixin' to get all the sense for himself by appointin' himself caretaker.

The story was a close parallel to the Ashanti story Courlander knew so well. Through centuries of change, in a different language, Anansi the Spider had been transformed but had persisted in the oral tradition, appearing now as Buh Rabbit or Buh Terrapin. What struck Courlander most about black American storytelling was how it brought people together. Children would sit and listen as elders—grandparents or other relatives—shared the stories. The tales weren't just for entertainment; they were used to teach important lessons about values, proper behavior, and sometimes survival. This was related to patterns of West African community life and culture, where storytelling is used as a way of teaching and learning for the young and old.

Toward the end of his stay in the South, Courlander wanted to see if he could find some traditional musical instruments. One day, in a small cabin in western Alabama, he saw what looked like a storage bin. When he went closer, he saw that this was no ordinary storage bin. Rather, it was a carved, hollow-log drum. The skin had long ago

been removed, but its shape and carvings were unmistakably African. Once again, in the American South, he had found a connection, however changed by time and history, to the vital culture of Africa.

▲▲

ALTHOUGH HE WAS making inroads in his field research, Courlander was dismayed by the racism and denial of equal rights and privileges to blacks that he witnessed continually. Langston Hughes acknowledged as much in this short note he sent to Courlander.

> Dear Harold,
> Thanks a lot for the lovely little book of Alabama songs with your kind inscription, which I find today on my return from a Southern lecture trip—a South all covered with snow—and so pretty you wouldn't think it could behave so badly. . . .
> Regards,
> Langston
> (March 14, 1960)

Courlander realized that he himself could not fight every battle against racism that presented itself, but there were times when he had to take a stand.

Once he was riding a train from Florida back to Alabama on the seaboard line. He made his way into the dining car, took a seat, and ordered his dinner. A few moments later, an older black woman and a young woman who appeared to be her daughter entered the car. One of the porters took her aside. "You'll have to sit over here," he told her. He led the pair to a table in the back, and then put up a screen, so that they couldn't be seen by anyone else in the car. Sit-

ting in the dining car at that moment, Courlander resented it. He took it personally, as an an insult to himself and everything he believed in. Quietly, he walked over to the table behind the screen. "Would you mind very much," he asked the woman, "if I were to sit and eat my dinner here with you and your daughter?" She was a bit surprised, but she agreed. He went over to the waiter and told him, "I'll be eating my dinner over there with those two ladies." Everyone was a little nervous at first, but his food was delivered and the meal went along without a problem.

"That was my protest," Courlander said. "I don't know if anybody noticed. Nobody said anything. But I lived by that code, and the people in that car didn't mind."

Courlander's work in the South resulted in a rich collection of writings and recordings, from his study *Negro Folk Music U.S.A.* to the folktale collection *Terrapin's Pot of Sense* to *The Big Old World of Richard Creeks.* Rich Amerson and Earthy Anne, Red Willie, and other singers can still be heard on Folkways recordings, including an early version of the famous ballad "John Henry," which, as Rich says on the album, comes "direct from the mountains." Courlander's work there represents a substantial contribution to the legacy of African-American folksong, folklife, and social history of the 1950s.

CHAPTER 8

A VOICE FOR THE PEOPLE

IN 1954, COURLANDER LEFT HIS WORK as a news analyst with the Voice of America when he became a press officer and speechwriter for the United Nations. He and Emma lived in New York City. Their son, Michael, was born in 1951 and their daughter, Susan, was born four years later. In the years immediately following World War II, the United Nations symbolized humanity's hope for lasting peace. As a journalist who had traveled to many parts of the world, Courlander could now see how people tried to solve problems of war, hunger, and disease on an international scale as representatives of nations new and old met in the General Assembly. His book *Shaping Our Times: What the United Nations Is and Does* describes much of what he learned and observed.

The 1960s into the '70s was a time of great productivity for Courlander in his own writing as well. He was becoming known more and more as an authoritative scholar and writer in the field of oral

Emma Meltzer, Courlander's second wife, with Michael and Susan (left), in Port-au-Prince, 1958. *(Photo: Harold Courlander. Courtesy Courlander Family)*

literature and cultural studies. He wrote folktales and anthologies, fiction and nonfiction, and he produced records and spoke as a radio commentator on current events. It was a time for him to bring to the world the wealth of stories he had been documenting and absorbing for so many years.

Courlander had lived in Haiti and Ethiopia, he had traveled to India and other parts of Asia, he had traced the roots of Africans in the Americas with visits to Ghana and Nigeria, and he had collected songs and stories in the South. Now he was ready to transform what he had learned from the oral tradition into the printed word. A collection of African folktales, *The Cow-Tail Switch and Other West African Stories,* that he co-wrote with anthropologist George Herzog had already won a prestigious Newbery Honor in 1947. There followed *The King's Drum and Other African Stories, The Piece of Fire and*

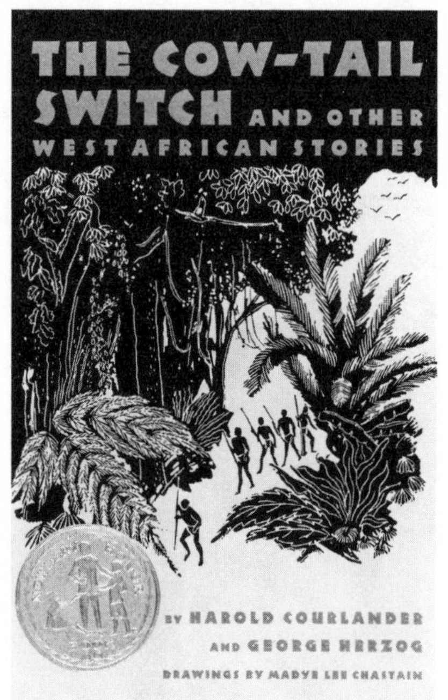

Left: *The Tiger's Whisker,* Courlander's collection of Asian tales, first published in 1959. *(Courtesy Courlander Estate)* Right: *The Cow-Tail Switch and Other West African Stories,* one of Courlander's most well known folktale collections, first published in 1947. *(Courtesy Henry Holt and Company, Inc.)*

Other Haitian Tales, The Tiger's Whisker and Other Tales from Asia and the Pacific, The Hat-Shaking Dance and Other Ashanti Tales from Ghana, and *Olode the Hunter and Other Tales from Nigeria.*

Courlander had always followed his own path, and through his investigations had gained insights into life and people. Now he was acting as a voice for all the people who had shared their stories, their songs, and their lives with him. During this period, Courlander could not always travel to the places where the stories came from, such as Indonesia, China, and Korea. He collected many of these stories from informants, people of different cultural backgrounds who were then living in the United States, as well as from translations of ancient texts and earlier anthropologists' fieldwork.

Courlander felt a deep responsibility to the people whose stories he had collected and was now retelling. Sometimes he had to defend the style or content of the folktales to editors he worked with. In one collection, there was a Hottentot tale. "It was about how people die and don't live again. That was the theme of it—how that came about. It was a kind of 'how it began' story, why after people die they don't live again. An editor I was dealing with said, 'A lot of people don't believe that, they believe you do live again.' And I had to be adamant about it and say, 'This is the story!' The editor didn't think it was suitable for children. Well too bad, they have to learn other people don't think the same way as they do—that's what it's all about."

Courlander's own family was from Central and Eastern Europe. He himself had grown up a second-generation American in the Midwest. Yet he felt impelled to record, write, and interpret what he had learned in Haiti, Ethiopia, Asia, and West Africa. As much as he was a writer, Courlander was also a great consummate listener. His ear for music, for language, for nuance and inflection, his curiosity about black American stories, dating back to his childhood in

Detroit, had taken him on a lifelong journey into world culture. "I always felt, this material is oral literature. Even before I ever heard the term, I felt it was literature. It was a product of a culture and it had to be properly represented in as simple and straightforward a way as possible without a lot of changes."

Courlander knew that, unlike written literature, stories from the oral tradition had different versions, that storytellers often changed them as they were passed from one generation to the next and from one language to another. How did he find a way to choose from among these tales? How could he write them so that, to the reader, they would feel as true to their origins as possible? He once said, "I've always been sensitive to hearing, and to sort of taking it in. You can't just sit down and knock off a story. If you have a feeling for the actuality of the people, it helps a lot. I've had stories told to me, where I didn't quite follow the punchline. A lot of Haitian stories that derive from Africa, for example, may have lost a particular element in transmission down the generations. Maybe their fathers and mothers got the point. If I wasn't sure about the meaning of a story, I generally pursued it till I got other sources. Then in some cases, I would combine what I knew when I retold them. The second source gave me what I was missing, I guess I have saved a few from oblivion. I'm glad of that. It's been fun. It's not been just for somebody else—I got a lot of enjoyment out of it, and out of meeting and working with the people themselves."

Courlander could see the modern world coming to all the countries he visited. He knew that these oral traditions were being affected by many forces, that stories would be lost. He felt it was important to preserve and record as much of the rich narratives and expressions he was hearing. Ever thorough, each of his books and recordings is accompanied by extensive notes giving background on

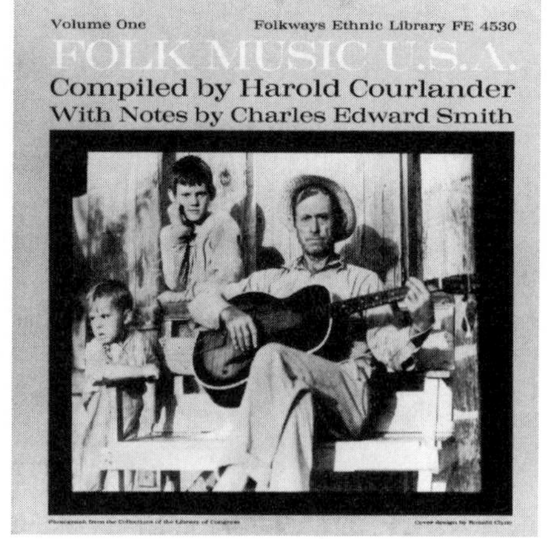

Left: Courlander conceived, edited, and narrated *The World of Man* in two volumes for Folkways, in 1956 and 1958. The sounds and songs of these collections reflect his interest in the common themes of the human experience. *Right:* A collection of American folk music from all regions of the country, produced by Folkways in 1958. *(Courtesy the Center for Folklife Programs and Cultural Studies, Smithsonian Institution)*

the geographical regions, the sources of the stories, the songs and the singers. He told me during our interviews: "I was always looking for a whole picture—not just the music or stories by themselves. Folklore is just a fragment." What was the whole picture? How did these patterns fall into place to create a sociocultural reality for one group of people? What did the songs and stories mean to the community that was transmitting them? These were the questions that concerned him.

In his experiences with publishers, Courlander often argued with editors who claimed that folktales belonged to the "young readers" category. In their cultural settings, the stories were a part of daily life and a way of educating young and old. "We think of folklore as children's literature, which it isn't, or wasn't, originally. It was for everybody. In African cultures especially, stories are . . . for older people and younger people. Everybody listens in. If the young people want an explanation, they get it from the tellers." In some cases he saw, storytelling sessions were informal, where listeners gather around a mother or grandmother. For special occasions, such as a wake, professional storytellers were called in to perform.

"With many African folktales as I know them, there was always a point to them. And they might end with a specifically worded proverb. Here is one that I used in *The Cow-Tail Switch:* This hunter left his family to go hunting. He didn't come back. Once in a while a member of the family said, 'I wonder where father is? I haven't seen him.' 'Well you know he went hunting.' And then no one would mention it anymore. A year would go by, and someone would say, 'You know, father never came back.'

"There's a baby, that's born after the hunter had left. He grew normally to a certain point, and just when he began to speak, his first words were: 'Where is my father?' And everyone said: 'Yes, yes, where is father?' and his sons said, 'Don't you remember? Father went hunting. Don't you think maybe we'd better go look for him?' The sons of the father went in search—each of them had a special capability. One of them had the gift of knowing directions . . . They said, 'Which way shall we go?' and the one who had the gift of directions said, 'I think we should go that way.' Eventually they reached the place. They found the skeleton of their father. He had been killed by a leopard or something. He'd been lying there. And they said, 'Oh, this is father. You can tell by some of the clothing items lying around. And that's his spear.'

"They didn't know what do to until one of them, who had the gift of putting flesh on bones, did something and put the flesh on the bones. Another one had the gift of putting the skin over the flesh. And still his body was lying there. Another one had the gift of speech and he gave it to the body. And the next one had the gift of movement which he put into the body. And finally the father was restored to life. He picked up his spear and they all went back home together. And of course there was a great celebration when the father turned up again—dancing and feasting and whatnot in the

village. The father was sitting on a chair, watching everything that was going on. And then at some point he said 'I have this cow-tail switch. It's made out of an animal tail.' (The handles were often beautifully carved.) And he said, 'I'm going to give this switch to that son of mine who did the most to bring me back from where I had been killed.'

"And the sons started a big argument and one said, 'I found it, because I found the direction' and another one said, 'But I put flesh on his bones' and another one said this and that. And after they had all made their arguments, the father turned around and gave the cow-tail switch to his little baby and said, 'He was the one. He said, "Where is my father?" He started it all.' And the proverb it ends with is: 'A man is not dead until he is forgotten.'

"You see how the whole story is built to lead to this proverb. And there are an awful lot of stories of this kind that lead to proverbs or sayings. Maybe it's not a profound proverb, maybe it's just a saying. In West African tradition there are many of those. Often in the process of transmission the proverb has been lost, you've just got the narration. . . . Many cultures are like that, the tales, with or without proverbs, are intended as educational—instructive is a better word—and in that sense they were directed towards adults as reminders, and to children as learning things. That's why the stories stayed alive, because they remained pertinent. That's why people kept telling them. . . . But then a lot of stories are instructive in different ways, not in moral terms, but as a way for people to ask questions. How did certain things begin? That's a natural question that is often thought-provoking. Where did we come from? Why are we here? So there's a story that will explain how we got here—and why certain things exist in the tradition. That's explained in the story too. The story either implies an answer or gives you a specific answer."

Courlander paid close attention not only to the stories he heard, but to how they were told. But can one person ever completely "take on the voice" of another culture? Or even of another person? Was it right for him to write in the voice of a black American, a Haitian, a West African? For Courlander, this was not a purely abstract or philosophical question. His writing style and personal values were directly shaped by his experiences with people from different cultures, as he knew and understood them. Overall, his love of story and narrative drew him to learn about these different worlds and to feel the need to express their way of life. But the field of anthropology had also seriously influenced Courlander. He was never an academic scholar. He never taught at a college or university, yet he had received grants and fellowships for his reseach.

Courlander had studied and corresponded with the great anthropologists of his time—Melville Herskovits, Franz Boas, William Bascom. And, as usual, he always came to his own conclusions.

Courlander believed that human beings are shaped most of all by their culture, not their race. In Cuba in the 1930s and 1940s, he had seen in certain ceremonies how "white Cubans"—people of European ancestry—had danced and played music with the same movement, rhythmic coordination, and even vocal styles as Cubans who were directly descended from African forebears. How was it possible for these modes of expression to pass from one "race" to another? Courlander concluded that it was cultural experiences that shaped these expressions. Due to historical circumstances, people in Cuba from different racial and ethnic origins were interacting, and so, their ways of communicating began to influence one another as well.

Once he cited an example of Matthew Henson, an African American who had been part of an expedition to the Arctic. He stayed with the Eskimos and had a son with an Eskimo wife. When American

explorers met the son, they could easily see his physical difference from the other Eskimos. Yet his language, his way of moving and physical gestures, his attitudes and beliefs all identified him easily as a member of his mother's family and cultural group. What made him who he was were his life experiences, from infancy, among the Eskimo people—not his skin color or body type.

Courlander asked, "How do you build a shelter? You build a shelter out of the materials that are available to you. If the Eskimos lived in Africa they would have been building straw houses.

"People ask questions. Human beings are curious. We want to know why lightning struck a certain object. We have our own explanations. Sometimes we can't really explain why it hit that house and not this house. Why did the lightning strike? Different cultures have different answers. But I don't find that Haitian or West African answers are anything more fantastic than what you find in the New Testament or the Old Testament, at all. It's just what people have been able to answer based on their life experience. I became more interested in the similarities rather than the differences among human beings."

The idea of the underlying unity of humanity was to remain a lifelong conviction, despite his acute awareness of social conflicts on the local, national, and global levels. In 1960, he brought these thoughts together in a pamphlet he wrote for the Anti-Defamation League—*On Recognizing the Human Species.* In the last chapter, he wrote: "All the peoples of the earth are members of a single biological species. Whether they live in great political states or in tribal semi-isolation, whether they are adherents to one of the great modern religions or of so-called 'pagan' beliefs, whether they specialize in making mechanical devices or in raising cattle, all people are representatives of *Homo sapiens.* No living example of an early inferior species of man has ever been found. . . . Societies develop or remain

undeveloped according to the dynamics of their needs, their wishes, their surroundings, and their dreams. All societies build their institutions and their way of life out of the common materials of the earth and their common human impulses. . . . Between one group of people and another, regardless of their particular solutions [to] the problems of living, it is impossible to distinguish varying degrees of human nature. Just below the surface of manners and customs lies our common identity." Perhaps it was this sense of common humanity that, even unconsciously, also drew him to explore and write in cultural voices that were not his "own."

In 1960, Courlander left his work with Folkways and the United Nations to return to journalism and broadcasting with the Washington office of the Voice of America. He moved with Emma and their children to Bethesda, Maryland, which became their hometown. The year 1960 also saw the publication of his masterwork on Haiti, *The Drum and the Hoe: Life and Lore of the Haitian People.* Courlander had been making trips to Haiti since the early 1930s. In *The Drum and the Hoe,* he put his years of work, learning, and love of Haitian culture into one comprehensive volume. The book was a way for Courlander to give voice to the richness and complexity of life in Haiti. As a scholarly resource, this work also established him as an authority in the field of cultural studies and made his name known to a wider audience.

Although Courlander worked in many fields—anthropology, folklore, ethnomusicology—he always saw himself, first and foremost, as a writer, a narrator, a storyteller. Writing fiction was his way to express and assimilate what he had come to understand and feel about the people and ways of life he had encountered. For Courlander, the ethnographic documentation and field studies were never enough. If he felt he had really gotten a picture, a feel for "the inner

Cover of the first edition of *The Drum and the Hoe: Life and Lore of the Haitian People.* Published to high critical acclaim in 1960, it is still considered a classic in the field. *(Courtesy Courlander Estate)*

culture" of a people, then characters and motifs would form in his own head and had to be expressed, not in a rigorous academic form, but in novels and fiction. "I'm ready to write when I'm through with the research, when the main study is over. There's a period of pondering. Questions would come to my mind. Working on a novel is a way of organizing everything through the literary approach—no holds barred."

In the early 1960s, Courlander began to be haunted by a character who was slowly beginning to take shape in his mind. What did it mean, he wondered to himself, for a first-generation African in America, brought over on a slave ship, to have to survive and adapt

to life on a plantation? What would happen to a slave's sense of self, his sense of language, his sense of his own destiny, in undergoing these horrific challenges? As the character became clearer, Courlander began to write of a young boy from Dahomey named Hwesuhunu. He saw him, in his mind's eye, working in the bush with his father and the other men of the village. He saw the brutal raid by the chief's men and the enforced march to the stockade in Cotonou. As he saw all these things, he began to write, and slowly a novel emerged. He called it *The African*.

In Haiti, Courlander had seen the potency of the African gods, the *lwa,* ever-present in the life of the Haitian countryside. He remembered Legba, the Dahomean god of fate and change. Legba of the crossroads, who had to be acknowledged and whose blessings were invoked before any journey. In the South, he had seen the church services and heard the proverbs, listened to the songs played on the banjo and strummed and drummed at weddings, funerals, and social gatherings. The services were Christian, but in all of them, he had heard the inner voices of Africa. Behind much of Courlander's thinking a theme began to resonate with great force and urgency: How would this young man find his sense of self and identity—cut off, as it must have happened, from his family, his village, his country, all that he knew and understood to be real, good, and true?

Courlander began to explore all these questions through the life of Hwesuhunu, who is renamed Wes Hunu by an old slave. In the novel, Wes eventually escapes from the plantation. Hiding out with his friend Julian among the Creek Indians in the Alabama woodlands, he thinks over all the things that have happened to him:

> Wes lay that night upon a bed of skin and blankets, but he could not sleep . . . Was Wes Hunu, who now slept in the Indian house, the

same person as Hwesuhunu, the African? For the things he knew most closely seemed to belong to another place and another time. . . . It suddenly seemed ridiculous to cling to the past. For here in this land there was no such thing as Fon, only white men, black men, and brown men. . . . Lying silently in the night he summoned up an old village song and sang it inside his head. But did this prove that Yabo ever existed? It proved nothing more than did an Indian hunter's imitation of the call of a groundhog. For to live was to communicate, as the drummer did to the dancers, as the Legba priest did to Legba, as the storyteller did to the people, as the dead did, on occasion, to the living. . . . Speech alone is not communication. For did not Julian and Vespey speak together without understanding? Nor could they ever, for they shared no common soul between them. . . . But what Wes remembered as the soul of the Fon, the thing he clung to that had given him the only certainty he had known, was it real or only a trick of the mind? And while he lay there and thought of these things and sought desperately for his identity, he felt an object like a sharp stone pressing against his chest. . . . It was not a stone, but the brass casting made on St. Lucia, which Kofi had given him before going out to be hanged. He felt its contours with his fingers. It was real. It seemed to bring Kofi alive, and all those others who had fought and died on the island. . . . It brought the slave stockade in Cotonou to life again, and his father, and Adanzan, and the village of Yabo, and the kingdom of Dahomey. This crude brass figure of a man, born smooth and now discolored, was the testimony and the link. All those things that were suddenly real again after having seemed to die and fade away, they had molded Hwesuhunu. And he understood gratefully that Hwesuhunu and Wes Hunu were one and the same, that he was here in the Tsoaha town only because Mawu, the parent of all vodouns, had thus written it down. In the writings of Mawu were the magic of creation and the fate of all men. In Mawu's mind Hwesuhunu had been given his life, his character and his Fa. So it was. He slept.

Courlander had been familiar with contemporary black American literature since his college days. He knew and admired the work of Zora Neale Hurston (whom he met in Haiti), Langston Hughes, Ralph Ellison, and others. Years before, after reading *Native Son* by Richard Wright, he had expressed in a letter to Herskovits his desire to one day write a novel of black life that would be as true to the black experience as Steinbeck's *The Grapes of Wrath* was to that of Oklahoma migrant workers. *The African* was the result of his efforts. It was a deep and thorough exploration of what he knew and understood of African-American history and experiences.

Alice Childress, the black American novelist and screenwriter, wrote to him after its publication: "Dear Harold and Emma— Glad to hear from you! I'm sure you've been busy adding to your works, and beautifully. An artist, Tom Feelings, was telling me about you and how your book *The African* is really told from a black point of view—that you're the only white author who has captured all the dreams, strivings, etc. I was proud to tell him you are our friend. . . . Alice and Nat."

▲▲

THE AFRICAN WAS published in 1967. Later, in the 1970s, it became the center of a storm of controversy with the television serialization of the novel *Roots,* by Alex Haley. When Courlander first sat down to watch the television series, he was surprised by the many similarities he saw in the plots of *Roots* and *The African.* When he read the book, he realized there were many other similarities to passages and phrases from *The African.* Courlander decided to sue Haley for plagiarism. Because *Roots* had become so popular and well known, the case was covered in newspapers across the country. The trial took place in New York City in the fall of 1978.

Cover of the 1967 edition of *The African,* Courlander's novel of Hwesuhunu, a young Dahomean boy who is captured and sold into slavery in the American South. *(Courtesy Courlander Estate)*

After six weeks of arduous testimony, Haley and his lawyers approached Courlander and offered to settle the case. An article in the *Washington Post* reported that "Alex Haley acknowledges and regrets that various materials from *The African* by Harold Courlander found their way into his book *Roots*." Although there was financial recompense, for Courlander the issue was much more one of standing up for the creative integrity of his work, and this, in a sense, had been recognized by Haley and the court. "It's literary justice," he told a *Washington Post* reporter. "Not justice for the whole world, but for something creative I worked on. Something creative is the most precious possession I have."

Whatever the controversies about its use of sources and authenticity, there is no doubt that *Roots* has had a lasting impact on contemporary American culture. And even in this circuitous way, Courlander's work—his years of exploration, writing, and research—played a role in changing our outlook by helping us to recognize the importance of cultural heritage and family history in shaping who we are as individuals and as members of the larger society.

Toward the end of the 1960s, Courlander felt it was time to pursue another large research project in oral literature. Although he had spent many years studying African cultures, he had always had an interest in Native Americans, especially those who lived in the West. Perhaps this went back to his early years, listening wide-eyed to his father's tales of cowboys and Indians. He also had a sense that there were many stories that had not yet been recorded that could reveal much about Native American thought and culture. And so in the summer of 1968, his own sixtieth year, he and Emma, along with Michael and Susan, made their way out to the Southwest, for what would be his last great period of work in the field, among the Pueblo Indians, the Hopi people of Arizona.

CHAPTER 9

THE HOPI

COURLANDER MADE HIS CONTACTS and decided that he wanted to pursue his research on the Black Mesa reservation. Some time earlier he had made friends with a Hopi family and had helped them to send their daughter to school. It was through this family that he entered the Hopi community. The Black Mesa is the site of a number of Hopi villages, the largest of which is called Oraibi. Oraibi is the oldest site of continuous settlement in the United States. It was settled in the thirteenth century by ancestors of the Hopi, the Anasazi people. The Anasazi migrated to Black Mesa after a great drought. They built towns and villages all along the Rio Grande, even into Mexico, making their dwellings in the cliffs of the high mountains. Because they lived communally, the Spaniards called them the Pueblo, "town people." The Hopi's name for themselves is "Hopitu," which literally means "people of peace."

Despite invasions by other Indian tribes, the Spanish, and then Anglo armies and settlers, the people of Oraibi and the mesa continued

to live and carry on their traditional way of life. Up to recent times, most of the Hopi lived in houses made of a hard clay brick called adobe. Women worked at pottery and baked *piki*—a flat bread made of cornmeal mixed with water. Men worked in the fields, planting and harvesting their precious crops of corn. Over generations, Hopi farmers learned to cultivate the dry desert soil and also raised melons and peaches and squash and pumpkin. Hopi families were grouped into clans. Each clan had its own way of identifying itself, taking its name from phenomena of the natural world: there is the Pine Clan, the Reed Clan, the Bear Clan, the Coyote Clan, and so on. As Courlander was to discover, each clan had a story of how it came to be named for a particular plant or animal. Each clan also had its own house of ritual and religious ceremony, called a kiva. There, the sacred myths and stories of the people are told and reenacted by the initiated members of the clan. But even outside of the kiva, the Hopi way of life is guided by its myths and spiritual beliefs. In the twentieth century, much of Hopi life had changed, with pressure from missionaries and government agents, and the incursion of the white world. Still, many of the ways of life and traditions were preserved and are still a part of everyday life. It was in this world that Courlander hoped to gain insight and understanding as he rode with his family in a jeep up the dusty roads to the reservation in the hot blazing sun of the summer of 1968. He was to make that journey many more times over the next twelve years before his work would be completed.

The first thing that he had to do was to find a place to live. He decided to start out in the village of Moencopi, the home of the family he had come to know in previous months—Uwaikwiota and his wife, Taskatama. He found an abandoned trading post at the far end of the reservation. It was an old building that had been deserted for a long time. But the Courlanders spent some time

making it fit and suitable to to live in, and then he could begin to do his work.

The first people he spoke to were his friends Uwaikwiota and Taskatama. They were very hospitable, and in a few days, they sat down with him and told him many stories, all of which he recorded. But after a while, he understood that these stories were ones that everyone knew and that everyone could speak of. There were other stories that would require much patience on his part, and trust on the part of the Hopis, to hear and learn. Stories among the Hopi are considered property, like horses or goats. And even more than livestock, they carry special value, for they are sacred. In some cases, each clan had its own version of a creation myth or the origin of corn, and even among the kivas, these stories were not shared. Sometimes outsiders—anthropologists or short-term visitors—had heard stories and then published them, without permission of the Hopi tellers. Sometimes the stories they wrote in English were not correct and misrepresented their true meaning. This was one of the obstacles that Courlander had to face in his quest to learn Hopi mythology and oral literature. Another obstacle came from within the Hopi community itself, especially in the town of Oraibi.

▲▲

AROUND THE TURN of the century, in 1906, there was a strong move on the part of the U.S. government to "assimilate" Native Americans into the Anglo way of life. Pressure was brought on the Hopi, already living on reservations, to change their beliefs and practices. Courlander tells it this way: "The Anglos were determined these kids had to go to school. Why did they have to go to school? They had to learn all the right way of behavior. They had to learn the American culture.

That's what the Hopi had to go through. They had to get their hair cut so they would look like 'real Americans.' They had to learn the English language. They wouldn't let them speak Hopi in the schools. They would be penalized if they spoke the Hopi language. The whole thing was to transform them into 'Christian Americans.' In Oraibi, some of the people were willing to cooperate, but another group was against it. The population was divided up into pro-Anglo and anti-Anglo. Sometimes they called them the Friendlies and the Hostiles."

But the Hopi were a peaceful people. They could not bring this internal conflict into an out-and-out battle. Instead they reenacted one of the scenes from their ancient myths. "They had a contest between the Hostiles and the Friendlies, and whoever lost had to get out of the village forever. It wasn't a tug-of-war, it was a push-of-war. The Friendlies all got onto one side, the Hostiles all got on the other side. They drew a couple of lines. And if they could push the other, pull them over the line over there or over here, then the other side lost." Due to the conflict, the town split. The Friendlies, or Progressives, lived in the Upper Village. The Traditionalists, or Hostiles, lived in the Lower Village.

A few days after Courlander had begun his research, his friend Uwaikwiota came up to him and said, "I almost decided not to help you anymore." Courlander was surprised. "Why?" he said, for he thought everything had been going well.

"I saw you talking to a man from the Upper Village. He is working for the Progressives. I don't have anything to do with him." And he told the history of the breakup of Oraibi.

When Courlander understood, he nodded and explained that he had only been talking with the man about general things—where to locate places in the village, where roads led, that sort of thing. Finally

his friend relaxed, and later he introduced him to some of the elders in the clan—people who remembered the most about the old ways and the ancient tales. Courlander realized that these were the subtle things that he had to understand if he was going to be able to communicate well in this different culture.

Courlander began to learn more about the Hopi mythology. He succeeded in gaining the trust of members of different clans. As he began to record their legends, he saw that although some of the stories were shared, there were also variations. No one's sacred myth was considered the absolute truth, yet each one had special meaning to its tellers.

Slowly, by listening to their stories, he came to understand more of the traditional Hopi way of thinking. He heard many different accounts, for different clans had different, and sometimes even conflicting, versions of their creation myths, even though certain elements

Cover of *People of the Short Blue Corn,* Courlander's collection of Hopi tales and legends for young readers. Courlander gathered these stories during his field research in northern Arizona in the 1970s. *(Courtesy Courlander Estate)*

were common among them all. Courlander retold these creation myths in his books *The Fourth World of the Hopis* and *People of the Short Blue Corn: Tales and Legends of the Hopi Indians.* He opens *The Fourth World of the Hopis* with the myth "The Four Worlds," which tells how the Hopi emerged into the world we live in today.

In the beginning there was only Tokpella, Endless Space. Nothing stirred because there were no winds, no shadows fell because there was no light, and all was still. Only Tawa, the Sun Spirit, existed, along with some lesser gods. Tawa contemplated on the universe of space without objects or life, and he regretted that it was so barren. He gathered the elements of Endless Space and put some of his own substance into them, and in this way he created the First World. There were no people then, merely insect-like creatures who lived in a dark cave deep in the earth. For a long while Tawa watched them. He was deeply disappointed. He thought, "What I created is imperfect. These creatures do not understand the meaning of life."

[Courlander goes on to recount how Tawa calls his messenger, Spider Grandmother, to bring these creatures into the Second World. Now they are transformed into animals resembling dogs, coyotes, and bears. But they continue to fight with one another. Tawa instructs Spider Grandmother to lead them to the Third World.

In the Third World, the creatures become human beings. Masauwu, Ruler of the Upper World, sends them fire. But evil still exists. The chiefs assemble. First, they create a swallow out of clay, who they send up toward the *sipapuni*—the opening of their cave—to see what the Fourth World is like. He does not succeed. Next, they send a dove, who enters the Fourth World but sees no signs of life. Finally, they send a catbird, who discovers land and water but no light or warmth. Courlander then tells of their journey to the Fourth World.

As the people climb out into the new world, Yawpa, the mockingbird, assigns them a tribe and a different language. Spider Grandmother, the chiefs, and medicine men then take a piece of buckskin and construct a round disk. They sing it into the sky. It becomes the moon. They paint another disk with egg yolks and golden pollen and sing it into the sky. It becomes the sun.

One day, a chief's son becomes sick and dies. The people realize that a sorcerer has entered the Fourth World with them. She is discovered, and the people prepare to throw her back down to the Third World. She begs to stay. An old man speaks.]

"Good and evil are everywhere. From the beginning to the end of time good and evil must struggle against each other. So let the woman stay. But she may not go with us. After we have gone on she may go wherever she wishes."

So that was the way it was settled.

The time was drawing near for the people to leave the sipapuni *behind. Yawpa the mockingbird said, "There is something still to be done—the selection of the corn." The people gathered around while the mockingbird placed many ears of corn on the ground. One ear was yellow, one was white, one was red, one was gray, some were speckled, one was a stubby ear with blue kernels, and one was not quite corn but merely kwakwi grass with seeds at the top. The mockingbird said, "Each of these ears brings with it a way of life. The one who chooses the yellow ear will have a life full of enjoyment and prosperity, but his span of life will be small. The short ear with the blue kernels will bring a life full of work and hardship, but the years will be many." The mockingbird described the life that went with each ear, and then he told the people to choose. Even while he was talking the people were deciding. The leader of the Navajos reached out quickly and took the yellow ear that would bring a short life but much enjoyment and prosperity. The Sioux took the white corn. The Supais chose the ear speckled with yellow, the Comanches took the red, and the Utes took the flint corn. The leader of the Apaches, seeing only two kinds*

of corn remaining, chose the longest. It was the kwakwi grass with the seeds on top. Only the Hopis had not chosen. The ear that was left was the stubby ear of blue corn. So the leader of the Hopis picked it up, saying, "We were slow in choosing. Therefore we must take the smallest ear of all. We shall have a life of hardship, but it will be a long-lasting life. Other tribes may perish, but we, the Hopis, will survive all adversities." Thus the Hopis became the people of the short blue corn.

[As the Hopis prepare to leave on their journey, Spider Grandmother speaks to them.]

"Remember the sipapuni, *for you will not see it again. You will go on long migrations. You will build villages and abandon them for new migrations. Wherever you stop to rest, leave your marks on the rocks and cliffs so that others will know who was there before them. . . .*

You will learn about the forces of nature in your travels. The stars, the sun, the clouds and fires in the night will show you which direction to take. But the short blue corn that you chose at the sipapuni also will be your guide. If you reach a certain place and your corn does not grow, or if it grows and does not mature, you will know that you have gone too far. Return the way you came, build another village and begin again. In time you will find the land that is meant for you. But never forget that you came from the Lower World for a purpose. When you build your kivas, place a small sipapuni *there in the floor to remind you where you come from and what you are looking for. Compose songs to sing in your ceremonies that will remind you how the sun and moon were made, and how the people parted from one another. Only those who forget why they came to this world will lose their way. They will disappear in the wilderness and be forgotten."*

The Hopi were not the only people living in the area. The Navaho, too, lived in communities nearby, below the mesa. Early in

the morning, Courlander and his family would see the Navaho drive up in their pickup trucks to the trading post. The women would be dressed in woven skirts, wearing bracelets and necklaces of turquoise and silver. In the early morning light, it was a beautiful sight. Once, while he was staying on the other side of the mesa, near a small café near a place called Keams Canyon, Courlander had the opportunity to become acquainted with some of the Navaho, who, like the Hopi, normally kept to themselves. As a white man and an outsider, he would automatically be mistrusted. Whenever he went into the café, the Navaho ignored his presence.

Courlander told this story: "Every morning when I went in there, the Navaho kept to themselves. They weren't interested in bonding with any white outsider. I was sitting at the bar one morning and this character, a man named Polacaca, came over to talk to me. He worked at the café as the sweeper and cleanup man. He was actually related to some important people in the Hopi village, but he was also a bit of a clown and a cut-up. The Navaho usually chose to ignore him. That morning, he was sweeping in this little café, and I noticed he had a belt. It was a tooled belt with all Indian designs on it, obviously made by a resident Indian. So I called to him, and when he got close to me I said, 'Can you tell me where you got that belt? I'm very interested in getting a belt like that.'

"He was showing off in front of the Navahos. He said, 'You like this belt?' I said, 'Yes, it's very pretty. That's why I'd like to know who made it so maybe I can get one made for myself.' He said, 'You like this belt?' I said, 'Yes, I do.' He said, 'I'll give you this belt,' and he started to pull his belt off of his pants, and I said, 'No, no, don't do that.' I realized what he was doing, he was performing for the Navahos, and by this time his voice was a little louder and the Navahos were all looking around very solemn. They stopped talking among themselves; they were just watching the performance. And

when he was aware of this he really went to town, he said, 'Here, take this belt, I'll give it to you.' I said, 'No. I can't take your belt.' He said, 'When an Indian offers to give you something, you've got to accept it from the Indian, you can't say "No I won't accept it," that's an insult!'

"I said, 'I don't mean it as an insult, all I wanted was a little information, and now you want to give me your belt.' And he said, 'Why won't you accept this belt?' and he's taking it and pulling it further out. And I said, 'Well, I do have a reason.' He said, 'What's that?' and I said, 'Because your pants will fall down.'

"The Navahos broke out laughing. Polacaca sheepishly put the belt back in its loops. The Navaho said, 'Come sit over here with us.' After that, whenever I came in for breakfast, the Navaho greeted me and made room for me at the counter."

Little by little, Courlander began to understand more about the Hopi way of life. The first field trip in 1968 was followed by many more, lasting until 1980. He was not the first to take an interest in the Hopi. They had been visited by anthropologists and writers since the turn of the century. One of the elders he met, a man named Don Talayesva, had been the subject of a book called *Sun Chief: The Autobiography of a Hopi Indian,* written in 1942 by a scholar from Yale named Lee Simmons. At the age of eighty, Don was still spry and vigorous. He and Courlander had many discussions about Oraibi village, and Don was able to tell him many stories and legends.

▲▲

ANOTHER OF THE PEOPLE that Courlander came to know well during his years with the Hopi was Albert Yava. Yava, whose true name was Nuvayoiyava, was a Tewa-Hopi. The Tewa shared the land of

Albert Nuvayoiyava, Courlander's close friend and research associate, in front of his sheepherding cabin near Oraibi, Black Mesa, Arizona. *(Photo: Harold Courlander. Courtesy Courlander Family)*

Black Mesa with the Hopi. They, too, had migrated years ago, from a village along the Rio Grande, and were related to the Anasazi people. Through marriage, many Hopi and Tewa families mixed and intermingled. Some Hopi villages were actually more Tewa, and some Tewa villages were actually more Hopi. Over a period of ten years, Courlander spent many hours with Albert Yava, listening to his knowledge of Tewa lore and to his personal stories and life experiences. Together with Yava, Courlander shaped these transcriptions into the autobiography *Big Falling Snow: A Tewa-Hopi Indian's Life*

and Times and the History and Traditions of His People. Through Yava's recollections, this book gives the reader many deep insights into Hopi traditions and the changes that the Hopi way of life had undergone in the twentieth century.

In one of our last interviews, Courlander offered to tell the following story. He remarked that it was one that he did not share very often, yet it must have held great meaning for him. In talking with Yava, Courlander learned that the Tewa of Black Mesa had migrated from a village called Tsewageh, not far from the New Mexico pueblo of Santa Clara, along the Rio Grande. The story of their migration from the village was one that was told in kivas of the Tewa clans, but no one had been able to return to the village since 1700. "They always regretted that they hadn't gone back." Courlander told Yava and Yava's son-in-law, Dewey Healing, that if he could, he would try and find the old site and photograph it.

In 1978, Courlander was on his way back to Black Mesa from the East. He had made an arrangement with his publisher that Yava would receive half of the advance for the book, and he wanted to bring it to him personally. On the way, he stopped to spend time in New Mexico, and as he had promised, he went in search of the old village:

"I went out, I did a lot of reading, looked at old maps and so forth, and had some verbal clues and oral clues. I located the site of Tsewageh, using as a guide a rough sketch map in John Harrington's book *Ethnography of the Tewa Indians* (1916). I went out and found the site of their old village, from which these guys had come to Hopi country. Of course there was nothing left there, no walls at all. In that particular village they had made their walls out of adobe, so a couple hundred years of rain and the adobe had washed away. But the site was obviously an old site. I went around and picked up pot-

tery and stone things and artifacts to bring them. I took pictures of all the surrounding country, and the features from which the village got its name, which meant 'A White Stripe Through the Cliff.' And I was just about to leave when I saw a kind of a round shiny stone from the middle of this old site. I went back, swept the dirt and found a very highly polished old stone maul, which was almost whole.

"I brought this all back to the Tewas, including the photographs. They were so delighted. It was the closest they'd ever come to the old place. It was like, 'This is our source, this is where we come from.' They were very unemotional, but I could see them putting that stone down and staring at it and staring at it—emotionally making connections with that stone that had come from their old abandoned village. And they studied the pictures and the photographs over and over. This endeared me to them. Then I went with Yava down to the local bank so he could cash his check. They play everything low key. They don't talk more than necessary. But a couple of days later, Albert and Dewey Healing came up to the place where I was staying. He felt a little awkward about it, but he said how some Hopis living down there in southern Arizona had initiated some Anglo, an honorary initiation. He still didn't quite know how to handle it because he had never done this before—he wasn't sure, he said, 'do you think that's alright? I don't think they should be doing that. Is that okay?'

"He couldn't quite sort it out, was my understanding. He said: 'Anyway, we want to initiate you in a Tewa kiva.' Everything flashed in my mind. I decided they wanted to do it because of appreciation—they wanted to do something in return for what I had done. I didn't want it that way. I didn't want them to have to feel obligated. So, in the Hopi way, I thought things over, silent for a while. Closed

my eyes. Finally I said, 'I don't think I can do it.' They said, 'Why not?' Immediately that was the reaction, why not? I couldn't explain to them my reason. I said, 'Because I don't think I know enough about your culture, and it wouldn't be right. Later on, when I know more, I'll accept the invitation, but not now.'

"So they accepted that. They thought it over and started talking Tewa between them back and forth, and they were very happy with my answer. . . . But we did compromise, they insisted I should come down to the kiva. Some of the older people of the village came down, we smoked. There was nobody down there saying, 'Put that pipe out.' We passed the pipe around in typical fashion, took four puffs and passed it on to the next guy. He takes four puffs and passes it around till the tobacco runs out, then you start all over. So there was no ceremony or anything. Officially it was not an initiation but I satisfied them. They were happy about that, too. We talked about a lot of things, they sang some songs. And it was an unscheduled event so they did whatever they felt like. They sang, they talked, they smoked, it was a very social evening."

▲▲

ONE BOOK THAT came out of Courlander's work with the Hopi was *Hopi Voices.* Here, he did no rewriting or retelling; he simply presented the words of the Hopi he had interviewed as he had heard and transcribed them. *Hopi Voices* represented a new stage for Courlander in his work of preserving and documenting the oral tradition, for in it he had stepped back completely as author and interpreter, letting the people themselves speak their own tales and history. The book found praise among the Hopi, who felt that their traditions

The cover of *Hopi Voices,* Courlander's collection of the legends and oral histories from the Black Mesa communities, first published in 1982. *(Courtesy University of New Mexico Press)*

had been represented accurately and with respect. In later years, he corresponded with his Hopi friends, among them Don Talayesva, Sun Chief. And Don always signed his letters to Courlander: "May your Guide keep your feet on a good and safe trail."

CHAPTER 10

REFLECTIONS

AN ASHANTI MYTH FROM GHANA tells how Kwaku Anansi, the trickster spider, brings all stories to the earth. Nyame, the sky god, has kept them locked in a golden box next to his throne. None of the great chiefs of the Ashanti, the Fanti, or the Akwapim can pay the price for his stories. But Anansi, using his wits and his cleverness, captures Onini, the python, Mmoboro, the hornet, and Mmoatia, the spirit of the forest whom no one ever sees. He brings these prizes to Nyame, and at a great feast, Nyame honors Anansi and presents him with the box of stories. When Anansi reaches the earth, he opens the box, releasing them, and stories have been running all over the earth ever since.

Today, in America and all over the world, the stories are still traveling. The stories have changed, as people change. More often than not, we read stories in newspapers, or watch them on television or at the movies, millions of us at a time, or bring them up on computer

discs and CD-ROMs. But at the same time, people are still telling stories to each other. Maybe they are not the stories we heard from parents and grandparents. Today's libraries are filled with folktales from around the world. Storytelling festivals draw hundreds, even thousands, of listeners. And in many places where stories are being told, in schools, libraries, or concert halls, you are likely to hear a tale from Ghana, Haiti, or the Hopi mesa—about Anansi the Spider, or Uncle Bouki, or a clever Ethiopian farmer. These stories have become favorites among tellers, teachers, and children, and so they are still being passed on from one person to the next. Often the teller will go back to the source and say, "I first read this story in a book by Harold Courlander."

Growing up in a century transformed by two world wars, by the invention of new and powerful technologies, some used for building and growth, others for destruction and terror, Harold Courlander made a great discovery. He found that in some parts of this ever-changing world, people were keeping an important part of themselves alive—by telling stories, by singing and dancing, by passing on their own unique histories, moral values, and spiritual beliefs so that their children, too, could be strong and survive.

In his way, he honored those people, the multiplicity of their voices, by saying to himself, This means something. It's important to remember, to write down, to record, to document, in the best way that I can.

Like Kwaku Anansi, letting out the tales from Nyame's golden box, like Spider Grandmother, traveling though the lower worlds and sharing her wisdom with the people, Courlander has played a part in keeping alive those precious threads of wisdom and knowledge. In his life's work, he was spinning his own kind of web, connecting us to our past, so that perhaps we could better see our way to a "good and safe trail" for the future.

A VOICE FOR THE PEOPLE

▲▲

HAROLD COURLANDER LIVED his last years in his family home in Bethesda, Maryland. His children—Erika, Michael, and Susan—were all married and living in different parts of the country and he had six grandchildren. In 1983, he published the novel *The Master of the Forge: A West African Odyssey.* It tells the story of a blacksmith, Numukeba, of the Bambara tribe, who leaves his home to take the path of the warrior and hero. Seven years later, Courlander wrote and published *The Bordeaux Narrative,* another novel. Set in the 1800s in Haiti, the book tells of a young man who goes in search of his brother, who has been taken away from his village by a mysterious sorcerer of the mountains. Courlander laughed when he told me that he wrote it when he realized that, after all this time, he had never written a novel about Haiti, the place where he had begun his first and most life-changing years of fieldwork. He opens the book with a poem:

Though we cannot see it
Do not say it is not there.
Though we cannot hear it
Do not say it is not there.
Ancestors, where they are living, cannot be seen.
The vodouns who protect us cannot be seen.
Our progeny waiting to be born cannot be seen.
Spirits within rocks and rivers cannot be seen.
Yet do not say they are not there.
What we see of the universe is a small leaf
Floating in a pond whose edges are beyond our vision.

Courlander did make one last trip to Haiti, in the summer of 1995, with his friend Roger Lyons. He enjoyed all of it—the sunshine, the

The cover of *The Master of the Forge: A West African Odyssey,* Courlander's epic novel based on his knowledge and research of Sudanic oral traditions and narrative forms, first published in 1985. *(Courtesy Courlander Estate)*

warmth, visiting old and familiar places he knew and loved, and discovering places he'd never been before. "Every time I go there," he said, "there is always something fresh, something new." He was still learning, still inquisitive.

At home, he continued to write, preferring his old "beat-up typewriter" (which he said had a spirit) to his computer. "If I sit down

to write and nothing comes out, I blame it on the spirit of the typewriter."

Born and raised in the Midwest, did he ever feel that the beliefs of the people he had worked with had become part of him? Courlander said, "I believe I got to be a sharer. The differences between people, that's only incidental. Anthropology began as the investigation of the mysterious ways of strange people. But I never found the mysterious cultures so mysterious. Whether tribal or industrial society, people are essentially the same—strip them of all the external differences, and what you have left is a human being with impulses, concepts of honor and dishonor, and what is right and what is wrong."

There is a common element in all the fiction that he wrote. From Tuesday in *Swamp Mud* to Wes Hunu to Wolde Nebri (the hero of his Ethiopian novella *The Son of the Leopard*) to Numukeba. Each character is searching—sometimes restlessly driven, at other times consciously choosing and following a path to find his destiny. "The search, the individual's search for something—the individual, trying to find the answers to knowledge. That is a theme which intrigues me." I asked him if this was not a mirror of his own life. Courlander said: "I guess I have been searching a lot. To some extent, I'm just another novel. It's just another story."

An Appalachian folk song says: "A story when it's telling, it has no end." Perhaps, too, the search has no end; we merely gain the knowledge that we have been somewhere, and learned something, as a new path opens before us. Perhaps it's only in the story that the truth of a person's life and purpose is fully realized. In *The African,* Wes tells a story to his friend Julian, a story he heard from his own father, of a hunter who goes out to track a deer. The path takes him to the land of the dead, and to a place where people have bodies but no souls. In the end, the hunter finds himself at a crossroads, where

Harold Courlander working at home in his study in Bethesda, Maryland, 1966. *(Photo: Michael Courlander)*

a skull foretells his future. He now understands that his fate is to continue the journey. Julian asks Wes: "Can this story be true?" And Wes answers: "Every story is true for one man. Maybe the man who tell it, or for everybody in the village, or maybe for someone not yet born. . . . I ask my papa, he tell me this: A story is like a feather blown around by the wind. Some folks see that feather and say, 'Oh, there's a feather that's all.' One day a man pick that feather up and weave it into his gbo, the thing that protect his house from bad spirits. The same way with a story. One day a man picks it up and makes it his own. Then it is true. . . . I think this story belongs to me."

IMPORTANT EVENTS IN HAROLD COURLANDER'S LIFE

1908	Born in Indianapolis on September 18. Reared in Detroit.
1931	Graduates from the University of Michigan, where his first play, *Swamp Mud,* had won the prestigious Avery Hopwood Award.
1932	Makes his first trip to Haiti.
1933–38	Lives with his family on a farm in Romeo, Michigan, during the Depression.
1937	Makes a field trip to the Dominican Republic.
1939	Marries his first wife, Ella Schneideman. *Haiti Singing* is published.
1940	Daughter, Erika, is born. Publishes his first novel, *The Caballero.* Travels to Cuba to conduct field research.
1942–43	During World War II, serves as the historian for the Douglas Aircraft Company in Eritrea. Records in the surrounding villages. Meets Haile Selassie, the emperor of Ethiopia, in 1943.

1944	Travels to Bombay, India, to work for the Office of War Information (OWI).
1946	Completes novella *The Son of the Leopard.* Joins the staff of the Voice of America as a news analyst.
1947	Works with Moe Asch and helps establish Folkways Records in New York City.
1948	Receives first Guggenheim Fellowship.
1949	Marries his second wife, Emma Meltzer.
1950	*The Fire on the Mountain and Other Ethiopian Stories* is published.
1951	Son, Michael, is born.
1952	Receives a grant from the Wenner-Gren Foundation to travel to Alabama to document and record African-American folklore.
1953	Receives second Guggenheim Fellowship for research and writing on Afro-Haitian culture and religion.
1955	Daughter, Susan, is born.
1956	Produces a six-volume set for Folkways Records, *Negro Folk Music of Alabama.*
1959	Publishes *The Tiger's Whisker and Other Tales from Asia and the Pacific.*
1960	*The Drum and the Hoe: Life and Lore of the Haitian People* is published to critical acclaim. Moves to Bethesda, Maryland, to resume job as a commentator for the Voice of America.
1962	Writes *The Big Old World of Richard Creeks,* a fictional ethnography.
1967	Novel *The African* is published. In 1978, the book becomes the center of a plagiarism trial after Alex Haley's *Roots* is published and later made into a television movie.
1970	Over the next ten years, Courlander spends time on the Black Mesa Reservation in Northern Arizona recording and documenting Hopi tradition.

1978	Records stories told to him by Albert Yava, a Hopi-Tewa elder; Courlander writes about Yava's life in *Big Falling Snow: A Tewa-Hopi Indian's Life and Times and the History and Traditions of His People.*
1983	Publishes his novel *The Master of the Forge: A West African Odyssey.*
1990	Publishes his novel *The Bordeaux Narrative.* Continues to write articles and memoirs.
1996	Dies at his home in Bethesda, Maryland, on March 15.

BIBLIOGRAPHY

Novels and Novellas

The Caballero. New York: Farrar and Rinehart, 1940.

The Big Old World of Richard Creeks. Philadelphia: Chilton Co., 1962.

The African. New York: Crown Publishers, 1967; Bantam Books, 1969, 1977; Henry Holt and Co., 1993. *ALA Best Books for Young Adults, 1969.*

The Son of the Leopard. New York: Crown Publishers, 1974. *ALA Notable Children's Book List, 1975.*

The Mesa of Flowers. New York: Crown Publishers, 1977; Popular Library, 1978.

The Master of the Forge: A West African Odyssey. New York: Crown Publishers, 1983; New York: Marlowe and Co., 1996.

The Bordeaux Narrative. Albuquerque, N.M.: University of New Mexico Press, 1990; New York: Marlowe and Co., 1997.

Nonfiction

Haiti Singing. Chapel Hill: University of North Carolina Press, 1939; New York: Cooper Square Publishers, 1973.

The Drum and the Hoe: Life and Lore of the Haitian People. Berkeley, Calif.: University of California Press, 1960, 1985.

On Recognizing the Human Species. New York: Anti-Defamation League/One Nation Library, 1960.

Negro Songs from Alabama. New York: Oak Publications, 1963.

Shaping Our Times: What the United Nations Is and Does. Dobbs Ferry, N.Y.: Oceana Publications, 1960.

Negro Folk Music, U.S.A. New York: Columbia University Press, 1963; New York: Dover, 1992.

Religion and Politics in Haiti (with Rémy Bastien). Washington, D.C.: Institute for Cross-Cultural Research, 1966.

The Fourth World of the Hopis. New York: Crown Publishers, 1971; Albuquerque, N.M.: University of New Mexico Press, 1987.

Tales of Yoruba Gods and Heroes. New York: Crown Publishers, 1973; New York: Fawcett, 1974.

A Treasury of African Folklore: The Oral Literature, Traditions, Myths, Legends, Epics, Tales, Recollections, Wisdom, Sayings, and Humor of Africa. New York: Crown Publishers, 1975; New York: Marlowe and Co., 1995.

A Treasury of Afro-American Folklore: The Oral Literature, Traditions, Recollections, Legends, Tales, Songs, Religious Beliefs, Customs, Sayings, and Humor of Peoples of African Descent in the Americas. New York: Crown Publishers, 1976; New York: Marlowe and Co., 1995.

Big Falling Snow: A Tewa-Hopi Indian's Life and Times and the History and Traditions of His People (with Albert Yava). New York: Crown Publishers, 1978; Albuquerque, N.M.: University of New Mexico Press, 1982.

The Heart of the Ngoni: Heroes of the African Kingdom of Segu (with Ousmane Sako). New York: Crown Publishers, 1982.

Hopi Voices: Recollections, Traditions, and Narratives of the Hopi Indians. Albuquerque, N.M.: University of New Mexico Press, 1982.

Tales and Oral Literature

Uncle Bouqui of Haiti. New York: William Morrow and Co., 1942.

The Cow-Tail Switch and Other West African Stories (with George Herzog). New York: Holt, Rinehart and Winston, 1947; New York: Henry Holt and Co., 1987. *Newbery Honor Award, 1947.*

The Fire on the Mountain and Other Ethiopian Stories (with Wolf Leslau). New York: Holt, Rinehart and Winston, 1950; reissued in 1995 by Henry Holt and Co. under the title *The Fire on the Mountain and Other Stories from Ethiopia and Eritrea.*

Kantchil's Lime Pit and Other Stories from Indonesia. New York: Harcourt, Brace and Co., 1950.

Ride with the Sun. New York: McGraw-Hill, 1955.

The Hat-Shaking Dance and Other Ashanti Tales from Ghana (with Albert Kofi Prempeh). New York: Harcourt, Brace and World, 1957.

Terrapin's Pot of Sense. New York: Holt, Rinehart and Winston, 1957.

The Tiger's Whisker and Other Tales from Asia and the Pacific. New York: Harcourt, Brace and World, 1959; New York: Henry Holt and Co., 1995.

The King's Drum and Other African Stories. New York: Harcourt, Brace and World, 1962.

The Piece of Fire and Other Haitian Tales. New York: Harcourt, Brace and World, 1964.

Olode the Hunter and Other Tales from Nigeria (with Ezekiel A. Eshugbayi). New York: Harcourt, Brace and World, 1968.

People of the Short Blue Corn: Tales and Legends of the Hopi Indians. New York: Harcourt Brace Jovanovich, 1970; New York: Henry Holt and Co., 1995.

The Crest and the Hide and Other African Stories of Heroes, Chiefs, Bards, Hunters, Sorcerers, and Common People. New York: Coward, McCann and Geoghegan, 1982. *ALA Notable Children's Book List, 1982. Parents' Choice "Remarkable" Award, 1982.*

PLAYS

Swamp Mud. Troy, Mich.: Blue Ox Press, 1936.

Home to Langford County. Troy, Mich.: Blue Ox Press, 1938.

SELECTED ARTICLES BY HAROLD COURLANDER

"Massacre in the Dominican Republic." *New Republic,* 93, no. 1199 (November 24, 1937).

"Plowshare Once He Turned the Sod With" (poetry). *Music Unheard: An Anthology of Hitherto Unpublished Verse.* Vol. 2. Edited by Margery Mansfield. New York: Henry Harrison, 1939, pp. 613–16.

"Chants d'Haiti." *Haiti Journal.* February 23, 1940.

"Musical Instruments of Haiti." *Musical Quarterly.* July 1941.

"Comparison of Afro-Cuban Cult Vocabulary with Efik and Congolese Words and Usages." For the Columbia University Archive of Primitive Music (unpublished). 1942.

"Musical Instruments of Cuba." *Musical Quarterly,* 28, no. 2 (April 1942).

"Profane Songs of the Haitian People." *Journal of Negro History* 27, no. 3 (July 1942).

"The Ethiopian Game of Gobeta." *Negro History Bulletin* 7, no. 1 (October 1943).

"Notes from an Abyssinian Diary." *Musical Quarterly* 30, no. 3 (July 1944).

"Gods of the Haitian Mountains." *Journal of Negro History* 29, no. 3 (July 1944).

"Abakwa Meeting in Guanabacoa." *Journal of Negro History* 29, no. 4 (October 1944).

"Dance and Dance Drama in Haiti." In *The Function of Dance in Human Society.* A seminar directed by Franziska Boas. New York: Dance Horizons, 1944.

"November" (poetry). *Saturday Review of Literature.* March 9, 1946.

"Incident in the Valley of Gura." *Negro History Bulletin* 10, no. 5 (February 1947).

"Many Islands, Much Music." *Saturday Review of Literature.* October 18, 1952.

"Music of Haiti" (monograph to accompany albums of field recordings). Ethnic Folkways Library, 1952. (Original album, Disc label, 1947.)

"Gods of Haiti." *Tomorrow.* Autumn 1954.

"The Loa of Haiti: New World African Deities." In *Miscellanea de Estudios Dedicados a Fernando Ortiz por Sus Discipulos, Colegas y Amigos.* 1955.

"Negro Folk Music of Alabama" (monograph accompanying six albums of field recordings). Ethnic Folkways Library, 1956.

"Three Soninke Tales." *African Arts* 12, no. 1 (November 1978).

" 'Roots,' 'The African,' and the Whisky Jug Case," *Village Voice,* April 9, 1979, and *Chicago Sun-Times,* April 29, 1979.

"Recording in Cuba in 1941." *Resound: A Quarterly of the Archives of Traditional Music* 3, no. 4 (July 1984).

"Recording in Alabama in 1950." *Resound: A Quarterly of the Archives of Traditional Music* 4, no. 4 (October 1985).

"Reflections on the Meanings of a Haitian Cult Song." *Bulletin du Bureau National d'Ethnologie.* 1986. (Actually published 1991.)

"Kunta Kinte's Struggle to be African." *Phylon* 47, no. 4 (December 1986).

"Recording in Eritrea in 1942–43." *Resound: A Quarterly of the Archives of Traditional Music* 6, no. 2 (April 1987).

"Reply to Aniebo." *African Arts* 20, no. 4 (August 1987).

"Some New York Recording Episodes, 1940–41." *Resound: A Quarterly of the Archives of Traditional Music* 7, no. 4 (October 1988).

"The Word 'Voodoo.' " *African Arts* 21, no. 2 (February 1988).

"Response to Consentino." *African Arts* 21, no. 3 (May 1988).

"The Emperor Wore Clothes: Visiting Haile Selassie in 1943." *American Scholar* 58, no. 2 (March 1989).

SELECTED ARTICLES

"Recollections of Haiti in the 1930s and '40s." *African Arts* 23, no. 2 (April 1990).

"Recording on the Hopi Reservation, 1968–1981." *Resound: A Quarterly of the Archives of Traditional Music* 9, no. 2 (April 1990).

"How I Got My Log Cabin." *Chronicle: The Quarterly Magazine of the Historical Society of Michigan* 26, no. 3 (1991).

SELECTED RECORDINGS BY HAROLD COURLANDER

All of the following recordings are currently included in the Smithsonian Folkways Archive Collection.

Music of Indonesia. Edited by Harold Courlander. Ethnic Folkways Library, FE 4406 (1950).

Music of Haiti, Vol. 2: Drums of Haiti. Recorded in Haiti by Harold Courlander; introduction and notes by Harold Courlander. Ethnic Folkways Library, FE 4403 (1950).

Negro Folk Music of Alabama, Vol. 5: Spirituals. Recorded in Alabama by Harold Courlander; edited by, introduction, notes, and text by Harold Courlander. Ethnic Folkways Library, FE 4473 (1950).

Folk Tales from West Africa. Told by Harold Courlander. Folkways 7103 (1951).

Folk Music of Ethiopia. Edited by, introduction by Harold Courlander. Ethnic Folkways Library, FE 4405 (1951).

Folk Tales from Indonesia. Narrated by Harold Courlander. Folkways 7102 (1951).

Cult Music of Cuba. Recorded in Cuba by Harold Courlander; introduction and notes by Harold Courlander. Ethnic Folkways Library, FE 4410 (1951).

Negro Folk Music of Alabama, Vol. 1: Secular Music. Recorded in Alabama by Harold Courlander; general editor, Harold Courlander; introduction,

notes, and text by Harold Courlander. Ethnic Folkways Library, FE 4417 (1951).

Music of Spain. General editor, Harold Courlander. Ethnic Folkways Library, FE 4411 (1951).

Folk Music of Pakistan. Edited by Harold Courlander. Ethnic Folkways Library, FE 4425 (1951).

Music of Haiti, Vol. 1: Folk Music of Haiti. Recorded by Harold Courlander; edited by, introduction and notes by Harold Courlander. Ethnic Folkways Library, FE 4407 (1951).

Music of Haiti, Vol. 3: Songs and Dances of Haiti. Recorded by Harold Courlander; introduction and notes by Harold Courlander. Ethnic Folkways Library, FE 4432 (1952).

Fabre Duroseau: Haitian Piano. Recorded in Haiti by Harold Courlander. Ethnic Folkways Library, FW 6837 (1952).

Calypso and Méringues. Recorded in Haiti by Harold Courlander; notes and translations (merengues only) by Harold Courlander, Folkways 6808 (1953).

Ring Games: Line Games and Play-Party Songs of Alabama. Recorded and edited by Harold Courlander. Ethnic Folkways Library, FW 7004 (1953).

Spirituals with Dock Reed and Very Hall Ward. Recorded in Alabama by Harold Courlander. Folkways 2038 (1953).

African and Afro-American Drums. Edited by, introduction and notes by Harold Courlander. Ethnic Folkways Library, FE 4502 (1954).

Negro Folk Music of Alabama, Vol. 6: Ring Game, Songs and Others. Recorded in Alabama by Harold Courlander; edited by, introduction, notes, and text by Harold Courlander. Ethnic Folkways Library, FE 4474 (1955).

Music of the World's Peoples, Vols. 1–5. General editor, Harold Courlander. Folkways 4504–4508 (1951–55).

Radio Programme III, Courlander's Almanac: Familiar Music in Strange Places. Radio program prepared by Harold Courlander for NBC series *Collector's Item*. Notes by Harold Courlander. Folkways 3863 (1956).

Uncle Bouqui of Haiti, by Harold Courlander. From the collection by Harold Courlander. Narrated by Augusta Baker. Folkways 7107 (1956).

The World of Man, Vol. 1: His Work. Story and narration by Harold Courlander. Folkways 7431 (1956).

SELECTED RECORDINGS

Africa South of the Sahara. Compiled by Harold Courlander. Ethnic Folkways Library, FE 4503 (1957).

The World of Man, Vol. 2: His Religion. Story and narration by Harold Courlander. Folkways 7432 (1958).

Folk Music U.S.A., Vol. 1. Compiled by Harold Courlander. Folkways Ethnic Library, FE 4530 (1958).

Ashanti: Folk Tales from Ghana. From *The Hat-Shaking Dance and Other Tales from the Gold Coast* by Harold Courlander. Narrated by Harold Courlander. Folkways 7710 (1959).

Ride with the Sun. Edited by Harold Courlander. Folkways 7109 (1959).

Folk and Classical Musics of Korea. General editor, Harold Courlander. Ethnic Folkways Records, FE 4424 (1959).

Modern Greek Heroic Oral Poetry. General editor, Harold Courlander. Ethnic Folkways Library, FW 4468 (1959).

Negro Folk Music of Alabama, Vol. 3: Rich Amerson, I. Recorded in Alabama by Harold Courlander; edited by, introduction, notes, and text by Harold Courlander. Ethnic Folkways Library, FE 4471 (1960).

Caribbean Folk Music, Vol. 1. General editor, Harold Courlander; compiled by, notes by Harold Courlander. Ethnic Folkways Library, FE 4533 (1960).

Tuareg Music of the Southern Sahara. Recorded by Finola and Geoffrey Holiday; general editor, Harold Courlander. Ethnic Folkways Library, FE 4470 (1960).

Jack Moyles: Hopi Tales. From *People of the Short Blue Corn* by Harold Courlander. FW 7778 (1971).

BIBLIOGRAPHIC NOTES

All references to Courlander's books, articles, and recordings are cited in full in the Bibliography and list of Selected Recordings. Additional sources used for background and general information are cited in the following notes.

1. Beginnings (pages 5–18)

I talked with Harold Courlander about his early years and school experiences during our interviews in April 1994, in June 1995, and intermittently during phone conversations. Portions of these personal memoirs are incorporated throughout the chapter narratives on pages 5–18. Michael Courlander was extremely helpful in providing specific details as to family history, names, and places after Mr. Courlander's death. *Something About the Author* (Anne Commire, ed. Vol 6. Detroit: Gale Research, 1974) provided an initial chronology. A chronology and vitae was also provided by Courlander during our first meeting. The staff of the Bentley Historical Library of the University of Michigan provided from their archives copies of *Swamp Mud* (see pages 15–17) and *Procession* (February 1931 and Summer 1932) (see pages 14–15), the literary magazine that Courlander edited during his undergraduate years at Michigan. To learn about folksong collecting and folklore studies in the first half of the century, I referred to P. K. Wilgus, *Anglo-American Folksong Scholarship Since 1898* (New Brunswick, N.J.: Rutgers University Press, 1959) and John Lomax's *Adventures of a Ballad Hunter* (New York: Macmillan and Co., 1947). Joe Hickerson, Director of the Archives of the American Folklife Cen-

ter at the Library of Congress, provided valuable insight into the history of folklore scholarship during the early years of the twentieth century when I visited the American Folklife Center in March 1996.

2. Haiti (pages 19–38)

The chapter on Haiti includes verbatim passages (see pages 19–21) from transcripts of June and July 1995 interviews. An excerpt from Courlander's article "Recollections of Haiti in the 1930s and '40s," appears on pages 22–24. My recounting of the Vodoun ritual (which is on pages 27–32) is based on Courlander's more detailed description from chapter 4 ("Rites at Léogâne") of *Haiti Singing.* I've also included a short excerpt from *Haiti Singing* (which appears on page 25) and a reprint of the story "Bouki and Ti Malice Go Fishing" (which appears on pages 34–35) from *The Drum and the Hoe: Life and Lore of the Haitian People.* Pétro and *Ibo* (which are mentioned on page 25) are distinct dance and music styles related to different families of *lwa,* or Afro-Haitian deities. Lucrece Louisdohn, storyteller and Assistant Director of Children's Programs for the Queensboro Public Library in New York, described aspects of Haitian folklore and the characters of Bouki and Ti Malice for my storytelling class at Bank Street College of Education in May 1996. Other background reading in Courlander's work I did for this chapter includes *The Piece of Fire and Other Haitian Tales, Uncle Bouqui of Haiti, Religion and Politics in Haiti,* "Dance and Dance Drama in Haiti," "Musical Instruments of Haiti," and "The Word 'Voodoo.'" Recordings of Afro-Haitian music I used include "Voodoo Drums of Haiti" (recorded by Richard Hill and Morton Marks, Lyrichord 1978) and Courlander's own records on Ethnic Folkways: *Music of Haiti, Vol. 1: Folk Music of Haiti* and *Music of Haiti, Vol. 2: Drums of Haiti.* The Caribbean Cultural Center in New York City (408 W. 58th Street) is an excellent resource for Haitian and Afro-Caribbean expressions through their ongoing exhibits and publications.*

* In 1979 the Haitian government recognized the use of the International Phonetic Alphabet for spelling Creole words. Prior to that time, Creole did not have its own official written language and used European spelling. "Bouqui" is the older, French, spelling, "Bouki" the more recent usage. In all cases we use current Creole spelling except when quoting directly from Harold Courlander's original publications.

3. The Farm (pages 39–47)

Courlander described his experiences on the farm in Romeo, Michigan (see pages 39–42), with me during interview sessions in June 1995. The excerpt that describes the storm, from his article "How I Got My Log Cabin," appears on pages 42–44. The song beginning "Jésus, Marie, Joseph, oh" (see pages 41–42) is reprinted, with Courlander's translation, from *The Drum and the Hoe: Life and Lore of the Haitian People.* This is a Haitian version of a children's game found in West Africa and other cultures in which players sit in a circle and pass stones to each other in rhythm with the song. Courlander collected many other children's games as part of his folklore research. (See Folkways recording *Ring Games: Line Games and Play-Party Songs of Alabama* in the discography.) Courlander's lifelong love of animals dates from this period (see pages 44–45). Michael Courlander provided confirmation of details regarding dates and names of family members. For further information on the Depression era, which I discuss on pages 41 and 46, the Smithsonian Institution's World Wide Web site on the Internet (http://lcweb2.loc.gov/ammem/wpaintro/wpafup.htm/) includes oral histories of American workers collected by the Federal Writers' Project in the 1930s.

4. New York and the Caribbean (pages 48–56)

Courlander related a number of stories to me about his life in New York in the late 1930s and early '40s during our interview sessions in June 1995. These included his thoughts about the Haitian massacre as his motivation to write *The Caballero* (1940) (see pages 49–50), and recollections of the Federal Theater and of the artists' community in Greenwich Village (page 52). The book *Trujillo: The Life and Times of a Caribbean Dictator* by Robert Crassweller (n.p., n.d.) and Courlander's article "Massacre in the Dominican Republic" provided more background on this epoch. An excerpt from *The Caballero* appears on page 51. Courlander also wrote about his experiences in New York in his article "Some New York Recording Episodes, 1940–41." The chapter "On Collecting Art and Culture" in James Clifford's *The Predicament of Culture: Twentieth-Century Ethnography, Literature*

and Art (Cambridge, Mass.: Harvard University Press, 1988) gave me background insight into cultural interactions in New York City in the 1940s. Background reading on the Federal Theater included *Hallie Flanagan: A Life in the American Theater* by Joanne Bentley (New York: Alfred A. Knopf, 1988). Selected correspondence between Melville Herskovits and Courlander was kindly provided with permission from Northwestern University Archives and by Robert Baron, Director of the Folk Arts Division of the New York State Council on the Arts, who researched this material for his doctoral thesis, *Africa in the Americas: Melville Herskovits's Folkloristics and Anthropology Scholarship.* Courlander's writings on his experiences in Cuba include "Musical Instruments of Cuba," "Abakwa Meeting in Guanabacoa," and "Recording in Cuba in 1941." For his story repertoire see the Afro-Cuban section of Courlander's anthology *A Treasury of Afro-American Folklore.* Courlander's recordings *Cult Music of Cuba* are a part of the Smithsonian/Folkways Archives collection. Many recordings of Afro-Cuban music can be found at the Latin Music Archive, Harbor School of Performing Arts, 1 E. 104th Street, New York, NY 10025. Louis Bauzo is the Director.

5. Ethiopia and World War II (pages 57–77)

Courlander related many of his experiences in Ethiopia, including events prior to boarding the *Château Thierry* and later at sea (see pages 57–61), during our interview sessions in July 1995. The excerpt describing Eritrea is from "Notes from an Abyssinian Diary" (see pages 66–67). Other references and material include "Recording in Eritrea in 1942–43" (see pages 63–65) and "The Ethiopian Game of Gobeta" (see pages 68–69). I also included several excerpts from "The Emperor Wore Clothes: Visiting Haile Selassie in 1943" (see pages 71–77). A reprint of the story "The Game Board" in *The Fire on the Mountain and Other Ethiopian Stories* appears on pages 69–71. Other references include the album and notes for his Folkways recording *Folk Music of Ethiopia* and *The Son of the Leopard*, Courlander's novella based on his knowledge of Ethiopian epic traditions.

6. Bombay (pages 78–86)

Passages from my discussion with Courlander about his experiences in Bombay (specifically pages 83–86) are taken from transcripts of our interview dated June 1995. An excerpt from Courlander's 1941 letter to Melville Herskovits (page 79) appears courtesy of Northwestern University Library Archives. The reprint of the folktale "The Scholar and the Lion" (see pages 81–84) is a story from the Panchatantra, the famed collection of Indian wisdom tales, that Courlander retells in *The Tiger's Whisker and Other Tales from Asia and the Pacific.* For a more in-depth look at the history of Indian civilization see *Indian Culture and Society* (New York: Oxford University Press, 1971).

7. Folkways and the South (pages 87–105)

Courlander's discussions in June and July 1995 provided much of the background for this chapter, which includes an edited reprint of the title story from *Terrapin's Pot of Sense* (see pages 101–3); an excerpt from *The Big Old World of Richard Creeks* (see pages 99–100); and his article "Recording in Alabama in the 1950's" (see pages 92–95). Album notes for his six-volume collection *Negro Folk Music of Alabama,* especially volumes three and four, provide extensive background on the storytellers, singers, and traditions he encountered. The song "Baby Please Don't Go," reprinted from *Negro Folk Music, U.S.A.*, is on pages 96–97. Another selection of songs was published in the collection *Negro Folk Music of Alabama* (New York: Wenner-Gren Foundation for Anthropological Research, 1960; Oak Publications, 1963). The Anansi tale of how wisdom came to earth (which appears on pages 100–101) is a summary of "Why Wisdom Is Found Everywhere" in Courlander's collection *The Hat-Shaking Dance and Other Ashanti Tales from Ghana* (1957). The letter from Langston Hughes (see page 104) is from Courlander's private collection.

Moe Asch and Courlander's relationship is described in an article by Tony Scherman in *Smithsonian* 18, no. 2 (August 1987): "This man captured the true sounds of a whole world." Courlander's correspondence relating to Folkways and to his work with Moe Asch, including the letter reproduced in

this chapter and the passage quoted on page 90, are part of the Smithsonian/Folkways Archives. For this chapter, I also read Zora Neale Hurston's *The Sanctified Church: The Folklore Writings of Zora Neale Hurston.* (Berkeley: Turtle Island Foundation, 1981) and Virginia Pounds Brown and Lauretta Owens's *Toting the Lead Row: Ruby Pickens Tartt—Alabama Folklorist* (University, Ala.: University of Alabama Press, 1981).

Recommended resources in the area of African-American folklore include Bessie Jones and Bessie Lomax Hawes's *Step It Down: Games, Plays, Songs and Stories from the Afro-American Heritage* (New York: Harper and Row, 1982); Linda Goss and Marian Barnes, *Talk That Talk: An Anthology of African-American Storytelling* (New York: Simon and Schuster, 1992); Linda Goss and Clay Goss, *Jump Up and Say! A Collection of Black Storytelling* (New York: Simon and Schuster, 1995); John Roberts's study *From Trickster to Badman: The Black Folk Hero in Slavery and Freedom* (Philadelphia: University of Pennsylvania Press, 1989); and Roger Abrahams's *Afro-American Folktales: Stories from Black Traditions in the New World* (New York: Pantheon, 1985).

8. A Voice for the People (pages 106–22)

Writings by Courlander that I used for this chapter include his nonfiction book and essay *Shaping Our Times: What the United Nations Is and Does* (1960) (see page 106) and the folktale collections *Olode the Hunter and Other Tales from Nigeria* (1968) (page 109), *The Cow-Tail Switch and Other West African Stories* (1947) (page 108), *Kantchil's Lime Pit and Other Stories from Indonesia* (1950), *The King's Drum and Other African Stories* (1962) (page 108), *The Hat-Shaking Dance and Other Ashanti Tales from Ghana* (1957) (page 109), and *Tales of Yoruba Gods and Heroes* (1973). A passage from *On Recognizing the Human Species* (1960) is quoted on pages 115–16. Relevant Folkways recordings include *The World of Man, Vol. 1: His Work; The World of Man, Vol. II: His Religion; Folk Tales from West Africa;* and *Folk Tales from Indonesia.* I also read selections from Courlander's news commentary with the Voice of America (1963–68), kindly provided by Michael Courlander. See Courlander's *The Drum and the Hoe: Life and Lore of the Haitian People* (1960) and *The African* (1967) for culminating works of this period. An excerpt from *The African* is on pages 118–19.

Courlander's retelling of "The Cow-Tail Switch" (see pages 112–13) and other comments were transcribed from interviews in June 1995. Additional readings about the controversy and plagiarism suit against Alex Haley (which I discuss on pages 120–22) include Courlander's " 'Roots,' 'The African' and the Whisky Jug Case"; "Kunta Kinte's Struggle to Be African"; news articles, including "The Roots of Victory" in the *Washington Post,* December 16, 1987; and *Alex Haley* by David Shirley (New York: Chelsea House, 1994). Michael Courlander kindly provided selected transcripts from the trial for research purposes. Further documentation of the trial can be found at the University of Michigan Library, Department of Rare Books and Special Collections. The letter from Alice Childress is from Courlander's private collection.

The question of authenticity and ownership in interpreting culture is a subject of much debate. Courlander had his own perspective. For insight into contemporary points of view at least as far as music is concerned, see Fred Ho's article "Playing Other People's Music: An Interview with Royal Hartigan" and "Playing Other People's Songs" by Anthony Seeger in Ron Sakolsky and Fred Wei-Han Ho's book *Sounding Off! Music as Subversion/Resistance/Revolution* (Brooklyn, N.Y.: Autonomedia, 1995.) Some of the opinions Courlander expressed in his discussion with me (excerpted on pages 110–11), as well as in his writings, are also outlined in "An Interview with Harold Courlander" by Diane Wolkstein in *School Library Journal* 20, no. 9 (May 1974).

For an all-around understanding of world folktales and folklore, see Stith Thompson's classic study *The Folktale* (Berkeley: University of California Press, 1977) and *Funk and Wagnall's Standard Dictionary of Folklore* (San Francisco: Harper and Row, 1972), edited by Maria Leach.

9. The Hopi (pages 123–37)

Courlander shared his memories and thoughts about his work with the Hopi during our discussion in July 1995. The incident with Polacaca and the Navaho (see pages 131–32) is also described in his article "Recording on the Hopi Reservation, 1968–1981." The breakup of Oraibi is also described

in *Hopi Voices: Recollections, Traditions, and Narratives of the Hopi Indians* (1982). I included an abridged reprinting of "The Four Worlds" from *The Fourth World of the Hopis* (1971) (see pages 128–30). Other works noted include *People of the Short Blue Corn: Tales and Legends of the Hopi Indians* (1970); Albert Yava's *Big Falling Snow: A Tewa-Hopi Indian's Life and Times and the History and Traditions of His People* (1978); and Courlander's novel *The Mesa of Flowers* (1977). For additional reading on the Hopi, see Mischa Titiev's ethnography *The Hopi Indians of Old Oraibi: Change and Continuity* (Ann Arbor: University of Michigan Press, 1972); *Hopi* by Suzanne and Jake Page (New York: Harry N. Abrams, 1994); and Leo Simmons's study *Sun Chief: The Autobiography of a Hopi Indian* (New Haven: Yale University Press, 1942). Recordings of Courlander's Hopi tales include the Folkways album *Hopi Tales* by Jack Moyles and Diane Wolkstein's *Tales of the Hopi Indians* (Spoken Arts, SA 1106). In working on this chapter, I am deeply grateful to Matoakah Little Eagle and her brother Powhatan Swift Eagle of the Thunderbird Indian Dancers for sharing the meanings of Native American traditions—including Tewa and Hopi music, dance, and story—in presentations to graduate students, staff, and children at Bank Street College of Education in 1995 and 1996. Other resources for learning about Native American cultures include the American Indian Community House, 404 Lafayette Street, New York, NY 10003, and the Resource Center of the George Gustav Heye Center; Smithsonian Institution National Museum of the American Indian, 1 Bowling Green, New York, NY 10004.

10. Reflections (pages 138–44)

For this chapter I drew on my own background knowledge of Courlander's story repertoire, including the retelling of "Anansi Owns All Stories" in *A Treasury of African Folklore* (1975) (see page 138). Core readings for this chapter include *The Master of the Forge: A West African Odyssey* (1985) and *The Bordeaux Narrative* (1990). Other noted works for his later years include *The Crest and the Hide and Other African Stories of Heroes, Chiefs, Bards, Hunters, Sorcerers, and Common People* (1982), and *The Heart of the Ngoni: Heroes of the African*

Kingdom of Segu (1982). I had the opportunity to discuss Courlander's last visit to Haiti with him during the fall of 1995. I am grateful to the poet Virginia Hardman of New York City, Courlander's longtime friend, for sharing her perspectives on his life and work with me during an interview in April 1996. A closing excerpt from *The African* appears on pages 142–44.

Major holdings of Harold Courlander's publications and recordings can be found at the following institutions:

Smithsonian/Folkways Archives
Center for Folklife Programs and Cultural Studies
955 L'Enfant Plaza
Suite 2600
Washington, DC 20560

Schomburg Center for Research in Black Culture
515 Lenox Ave.
New York, NY 10037

Archives of Traditional Music
Morrison Hall 117
Indiana University
Bloomington, IN 47405-2501

University of California
Ethnomusicology Archive
1630 Schoenberg Hall
Box 951657
Los Angeles, CA 90095-1657

Mugar Memorial Library/
Special Collections
Boston University
771 Commonwealth Ave.
Boston, MA 02215

Further Resources in Folklore and Storytelling

The National Storytelling Association
POB 309
Jonesboro, TN 37659

The American Folklore Society
4340 North Fairfax Dr.
Arlington, VA 22203

Archive of Folk Culture
The American Folklife Center
Library of Congress
Washington, DC 20540-8100

The Center for Folk Arts in Education
Bank Street College of Education
610 West 112th St.
New York, NY 10025

INDEX

(Page numbers in italic *refer to illustrations.)*

INDEX

INDEX

Franklin Pierce College Library
00152033